NO GHOSTS IN

NO GHOSTS IN THIS CITY

AND OTHER STORIES

Uddipana Goswami

ZUBAAN
an imprint of Kali for Women
128 B Shahpur Jat, 1st floor
NEW DELHI 110 049
Email: contact@zubaanbooks.com
Website: www.zubaanbooks.com

First published by Zubaan 2014

10 9 8 7 6 5 4 3 2 1

ISBN 978 93 83074 07 5

Zubaan is an independent feminist publishing house based in New Delhi with a strong academic and general list. It was set up as an imprint of India's first feminist publishing house, Kali for Women, and carries forward Kali's tradition of publishing world quality books to high editorial and production standards. *Zubaan* means tongue, voice, language, speech in Hindustani. Zubaan is a non-profit publisher, working in the areas of the humanities, social sciences, as well as in fiction, general non-fiction, and books for children and young adults under its Young Zubaan imprint.

Typeset by Jojy Phillip, New Delhi 110 015
Printed at Raj Press, R-3 Inderpuri, New Delhi 110 012

For Ma, Deuta, Majoni, Sunayan, Baba and Ritu – the people who saw me through my darkest days

CONTENTS

COLOURS

BLUE

Mor ee antar khani xagarar dare nila bedanare ...[*]
—Debakanta Baruah

This my heart is blue like the sea, with pain. I always thought I could feel this pain, this intense agony, deep down in my heart. I always feared this pain will be with me till the end, refusing to go away, which is why I decided I should do something about it, maybe leave it all and go away, far far away, from my parents, from all acquaintances, and from the familiar places that had shaped my life and given me this pain.

I was born in Guwahati, a city I called home but never really felt at home in. Many, like my parents, had come to this city from *mofussil* towns and villages to build a new life, and in the process, had started imparting to the city, just as the city had imparted to them, hypocritical middle class values. These were also the values that always repulsed me and instilled in me the desire to run away, to be someplace else, be someone else. I always blamed these values for my parents' lack of courage, the kind of courage one needs to be able to match up to one's ambitions. True, they capped their ambition at a stable job with a secure income, but it was a lot for them to achieve in a new city with a new way of life, and they were willing to do anything to achieve that ambition – provided it could be done without any kind of confrontation with anybody.

My mother was the more ambitious of the two; my father just sort of went along. He came from a very poor family that did not have enough agricultural land to be shared among the five sons, of whom my father was the fourth. So he had to come to the city to look for a job. My mother's father was a fourth-grade officer in the district magistrate's office, and he earned enough – very little of it by way of government salary of course – to keep his sizeable family of six daughters and two sons in relative comfort. She moved to the city when she married my father.

At first my mother was appalled by how little my father made at his job as an officer at the State Bank. What was more, he seemed content with his job and salary. But my mother had enough ambition for the two of them, and she forced him to sit for all the exams that would ensure him promotions, sitting up nights to ensure that he did the same, till he became a branch manager with a decent salary and the scope to earn some more on the side. After that, she used the influence of one of her father's acquaintances to join a government school as a subject teacher, and turned her attention to making something out of me. I was admitted to one of the three elite English medium schools in Guwahati at the time, a school that had a Catholic management and hence was sure to instill the kind of discipline she thought would take me far in life.

I was not an extremely bright student but good enough to keep her ambitions for me alive. Although I came to know early in life that she planned for me to be a doctor – because doctors are never without a job and make lots of money besides – I always wanted to be a writer. Even when I grew up and got to know that writers, especially in Assam, make almost nothing from their writing, I thought my parents had made enough – and then some – for me to live on for the rest of my life so that I could easily indulge myself and my passion for poetry and literature, which I had developed while still at school. But my mother would have none of that and she made me sit for the medical entrance test, which I cleared in the second attempt, thus falling behind my classmates and losing what little I had by way of friends and companions. But my mother persisted and when I did get through, I was so bad at studying medicine that I kept falling more and more behind in class. However, I did finally emerge an MBBS doctor and in the absence of any desire to pursue a specialisation, started looking around for a job, any job that would take me away from Guwahati and my parents and the ignominy of being the only one among my contemporaries who was not yet a specialist, gainfully employed, and married.

Finally one day, I got a call from the Kalguri Tea Estate authorities for an interview, and when I reached the tea garden and saw the bungalow set aside for the doctor and took a walk among the tea bushes for the first time in my life, I knew I had to get this job and come and live here. I did not care that in a tea estate, the frequently changing doctors are mostly retained for ornamental purposes, with the local compounder being the one the labourers all came to for the reassuringly familiar, high-handed, bumbling system of medication that he would have developed through years of trial and error. After all, I never did perceive myself to be qualified enough, having been always behind in class, and was only too eager to come to Kalguri to unlearn all that I had learned. For the first time in my life, on the night before the interview, at the tea estate guest house where I was given accommodation, I felt a kind of peace trying to make its way into my heart, nudging at the precious pain I had nurtured all these years. As I stood in the huge lawn and bathed in the naked moonlight, I knew if I came here, I would have all the time in the world to indulge my passion for literature, and read and write to my heart's content. As I looked out at the rows and rows of tea bushes in front of me, I could feel every novel, every poem, every word I had read about lives hitherto unknown to me, come alive and call out to me, entice me, irresistibly pull at every molecule of my being.

I did not waste any time after the appointment letter reached me. My mother said she would not let me go as far away as Delhi or Bangalore to study like many of my friends and cousins because she could never be sure whether I was applying myself enough, but I knew it was really because she could not bear to have me slipping out of her control. However, I was almost twenty-eight now, and could not bear to be near her anymore. I needed to break away, and even if it meant being only 400 kilometers away from her and lying to her that I wanted the effortless tea estate job so that I could prepare for my postgraduate exams and would be back in time for the exams in six months, I managed to get her to agree in the end. The fact that the tea company was paying me a very handsome salary must also have had something to do with her acquiescence.

The six-hour journey to Kalguri may not have seemed momentous in any way to anybody else; after all, there were so many people who travelled back home to Guwahati every weekend from what they thought of as punishment postings in Kalguri village, which had grown up around the tea garden, or in Barbari town nearby. For me, however, it was a remarkable journey, because for the first time I felt free, on my own and on my way to shedding the agonising blue that had housed itself in me all these years, so tenaciously, and it suddenly seemed to me, in hindsight, so melodramatically. And strangely, as the bus began crawling its way out of Guwahati, I saw the evening sun reflected in the waters of the vast Brahmaputra, and the fantastic blue of the sea neither I nor my poet had ever seen seemed already to be shedding its sadness. Instead, seeping into my heart now was the satiny blue of the Brahmaputra tinged with the red of the setting sun.

BLACK

Torou thakiba pare janu bhem
Naharani baganar koli mem...
—Pranab Barman

Can you too be so arrogant/Black memsahib of Naharani garden? I had come to Kalguri wondering whether it would turn out to be my Naharani, where I would find my black memsahib and a tragic love affair. I had been in love once, earlier, at medical college, but she had left me because of my lack of ambition as she perceived it. How would she know that I did have ambition – only it wasn't the kind she or my mother would understand? My ambitions were not limited to jobs or money; they had more to do with finding people, discovering places, and getting rid of all that blue. During my initial days at Kalguri, every time I saw a pair of muscular black calves below the undulating folds of a grimy sari walking away from me, I would wonder if she could have been my Chameli memsahib, and I – though not a white man – could be George Baker, shedding sweet tears of sorrow while in the background Bhupen Hazarika sang his heart wrenching, "*O Bidexi Bandhu....*"

But I did not fall in love in Kalguri, and all the black memsahibs gradually lost the romantic sheen I had draped them in. They became everyday people like their brothers or fathers or lovers or uncles, all of whom warmed up to me enough to soon start offering me their *haria* to drink and allowing me to participate in their evenings of *jhumur* dance once in a while. Alcohol had been taboo in our house, but now, having left behind the Hindu traditional universe I had been confined to, I got more and more attached to the drink. The more I drank, the more I rose in their estimation as somebody who was "not like the rest of them." Often I would get too drunk to walk back to my quarters on my own and a few of them would carry me and put me in bed. They felt good that the doctor sahib was fraternising with them, and no doctor at the tea garden had ever done that before. And I felt good that they were accepting me more and more into their lives, and often congratulated myself that I could shed my ingrained elitist education and upbringing to mingle with the workers and labourers.

I stopped going back to Guwahati every weekend like I initially used to under pressure from my mother. I also stopped calling as often as she would have me call her. My mother kept threatening to come down and stay with me, but I kept putting her off. My father made the appropriate amount of fuss, then gave up. My mother persisted, but I learned that it was easier to handle her long distance and mastered the art within a short time. All in all, my life at Kalguri was going quite well. I was leading the kind of idyllic idle life I had always dreamed was necessary for any kind of literary pursuit, whether reading or writing. Unlike many other tea gardens, this one had an excellent library, which had been built up over the years by the erstwhile white masters of the plantation, and I was catching up with all the reading I had missed out on in the years wasted in medical school.

When I wanted my dose of Axamiya literature, all I had to do was send one of my orderlies, Dambaru, on his cycle to the village headmaster Praphulla Narzary's house and I could have the learned man's handpicked selection of the literary masters. Whenever I was at the village, I would always visit him and discuss all that I had read with him, over cups of steaming tea or glassfuls of *jou* that his daughter, Deepti, had brewed. I would often cycle back to my quarters late in the night, despite Narzary *saar's* repeated warnings about gunmen on the prowl at that time. Every time I was late, he would apologise for not having kept track of the time, and plead with me to stay back at his house for the night rather than get shot by the militants or the army, whoever happened to be around. But the *jou* would have made me fearless, and happy like I had never been before, and I would ignore his pleas. Besides, as I always reasoned with him, it would not look nice if I stayed the night given that he had a young daughter at home, and nobody else.

Sometimes when I returned late at night from my trips to the village, which gradually became more and more frequent, I would find a potful of *haria* left at my door. No doubt by Dambaru who followed me around like a little lost black puppy most of the day, and at night missed me if I did not come to their *basti* to drink. Then I would drink some more of the *haria* or risk offending Dambaru and go off to sleep. No matter what time I rose, Dambaru would be ready with my breakfast. After breakfast, I would go off to the hospital. I would sit there as long as it took for the compounder, Biswas *da*, to have his paranoia come back and feel threatened by my presence and say kindly to me: "You must be tired, *saar*, why don't you leave? I can handle it here." Sometimes, the manager's wife who was nothing less than a queen in the tea garden would summon me to administer her insulin and I would spend a couple of hours talking to her about nothing of any consequence. And as soon as I could, I would return to my books or cycle down to the village or walk around to the labour *basti*. Once in a while, the manager or the assistant manager would invite me to come along with them to the Planters' Club where the management of about ten tea gardens in a radius of nearly two hundred kilometers would meet whenever they felt they needed the company of their peers instead of the illiterate uncivilised labourers they were forced to deal with day in and day out. I would accept the invitations at reasonable intervals but come back sick to my stomach with all their wives' flirtatious advances.

All in all, I was packing in more experiences during my stay here than I had ever absorbed in my whole life before. And I should have been able to write like I had always planned to, but I was too busy soaking it all in to find time to reflect and recollect. I was not complaining, however, and was perfectly happy with the way things were – till one day, I killed Dambaru.

YELLOW

Tumi mok bhal pale/Sarimuthi halodhiya xuta kini dim ...
—Jiban Narah

If you love me, I shall buy you four lengths of yellow thread. These lines always remind me of Deepti in her yellow *dakhana*, sitting at the loom, looking up and smiling at me every time I pushed aside the horizontal bamboo poles on their gate and walked in. How was I to know that Dambaru was in love with Deepti? How was I to know that Deepti – the college-going daughter of the village headmaster – could be in love with a boy from the tea tribes, an uneducated, quiet, mild mannered boy, whom I sent to her house so often at all odd hours to collect books for me? Surely it was because of me that this could happen but other than

Narzary *saar*, nobody in Kalguri village was willing to allow that fate also could have had something to do with the development of this socially unacceptable relationship. It was now a matter for consideration by the village elders, and though the Bodo community to which Narzary *saar* and Deepti belonged was largely detribalised, it did still retain a characteristically tribal distrust of outsiders. No Bodo could marry a *harsha* or outsider. And what is more, Dambaru's tribe was not even indigenous to Assam. His grandparents had come from somewhere in the Indian mainland as bonded labourers to work in the tea garden and had settled here. It was to free their indigenous land from the occupation of outsiders that many Bodo youths had taken up arms today and if it should be known that a girl from their village had been involved with a tea tribal, the entire village would be in trouble.

I was present at the meeting and I could sense the fear as well as the anger. But because Narzary *saar* was well respected, they let me off with a small fine. Dambaru, however, was not so fortunate. He was found killed just outside the tea garden one morning. Nobody could or would say who did it. But everybody began to keep their valuables packed and ready in small pouches, ready to abandon the village at the first signs of trouble. Able-bodied men from the village started staying up nights on sentry duty. I was forbidden by the tea garden authorities to go to the village, and I could not also go to the labour *basti* anymore, because even though they did not openly accuse me of anything, I could sense that they felt betrayed somehow. Meanwhile, the news of Dambaru's death had made it to the newspaper as it had followed closely on the heels of ethnic clashes between the Bodos and the tea tribes in the adjoining district. The media predicted that ethnic clashes were imminent in the Kalguri area also. My mother read the news and decided I was to come back immediately. Two years was long enough to have wasted in a remote tea plantation and according to her, it was time I got out of this mess and came home to take stock of my life.

I told her I could not come. For the first time in my life, I was straight with my mother. I told her that now more than ever, I could not and would not abandon the people who meant more to me than anybody else had ever done in my entire life. The city meant nothing to me, and though I did not directly tell her this, I am sure she also understood what I left unsaid – that she herself meant very little to me. She, who stood for all that I hated: a limited life, constricting values, and a self-centered universe. As I stood my ground for the first time in my life, I suddenly realised that I myself had epitomised the things that I had hated all my life. What had I done for the garden labourers who had welcomed me into their lives so uninhibitedly? I had taken their affection for granted and not even rendered them the service for which the garden management had hired me in the first place. On the contrary, I had jeopardised their very existence. It was not as though I was not aware of the tensions prevalent between the two communities – even though remote, news does travel to Kalguri. And there had been ethnic clashes in the neighbouring districts only a month ago. Yet, I had sent Dambaru to the Bodo village over and over again, in order to satiate my own lust for literature. I had been blind to the growing affection between him and Deepti, because I had not paid attention to either of them. I was so engrossed in my discovery of Narzary *saar's* treasure trove of knowledge that I had become insensitive to the boy who ungrudgingly acted as my go-between and the girl who quietly looked after my comfort while I was engaged with her father. Had I only acknowledged their existence and made an effort to know them as people, I could perhaps have gauged the growing involvement between them, and helped them before things got out of hand. Who knows? And now I will never know because Dambaru is dead and Deepti cannot even mourn his death because if she shows any sign of mourning, the villagers will ostracise her father. As it is, they blame her and Narzary *saar* for the imminent attack on their village, although nobody says it openly.

The attack came one night. There were people with bows and arrows and some with guns. Two Bodo villages in the area were razed and twenty people killed. The same night, five tea tribe villages were also set on fire, and fifty people made to stand in line and riddled with bullets. Dambaru's *basti* was inside the tea garden and the management had received prior information about the date of the attack so they had shut all entry points into the garden and tightened security. Some said they even paid the militants not to deplete their labour force. Cheap labour was hard to find and any untoward incident inside the plantation meant losses amounting to hundreds of thousands of rupees every day. So Dambaru's *basti* was safe, but Deepti's village was devastated. And Deepti had disappeared. The survivors had to go live in a relief camp twenty kilometers away in Kalibheta.

Two days later, when the tea garden management allowed me to take the official jeep, I went to the relief camp. Narzary *saar* sat under a tree and would not talk to me. The other villagers met me coldly and told me nobody knew anything about Deepti. As I was coming back to the garden, my driver stopped by the side of the road to take a piss. There was a mustard field there, and it was all yellow with mustard blossoms. I thought I could see clotted black blood splattered over the yellow.

RED, GREEN, GREY

Issa hoi tar hatar ranga patakakhan
Jui huwar agate
Tat jen xeujiya xutare buta basi aki dim
Puwatit jak pata uranta maral ...

—Geeta Goswami

I want to snatch the red flag he carries/Before it flares up/And weave into it with green thread/A motif of a flock of maral/Spreading their wings in the morning light. Between file shots of the red and green flag of their organisation, the local news channel was showing pictures of Deepti in handcuffs. That was when I discovered that she had joined the militants after that night. She told me later that she was carried away by the attackers, who dumped her in a mustard field not far away from the village. From there, she was picked up by a group of men who did not seem to belong to either community, but were armed with guns.

They had raped her, repeatedly, and dropped her off near the army camp at Barbari and she had crawled her way to a nearby village, which luckily for her, turned out to be a Bodo village. There, she was nursed back to health and indoctrinated in the militant ideology. Because she was well educated, she rose quickly in the ranks and they used her for writing press releases and demand notes and communicating with the media. She told me all this when I went to meet her at the jail in Guwahati five years later.

After watching the news, I had spent a sleepless night, wondering if I should go and see her. In the end, I decided I should. It took me a lot of maneuvering before the jail officials allowed me to meet her, but I managed somehow and I am glad that I did. She also seemed genuinely glad to see me. She told me how she had been away taking military training in the hills of Karbi Anglong when her father had died. She had gone to see him when she came back two years after the carnage, but he was no more. When I asked her why she had joined the militants, she said it was because she had been very angry. When I asked her why she had joined the very people who had killed Dambaru, she did not reply. Instead she asked me what I had been up to. I told her how I had taken the easy way out and escaped to the city. My mother had said nothing, but I knew she felt triumphant when I sat for the Assam public service exams and qualified and asked my father for money to pay for a post in the Guwahati Medical College. I had been leading a quiet life since then and next month, I was getting married to a girl my parents had found for me.

She said she was very happy for me. I asked her if she intended to surrender now that the government was paying generous rehabilitation packages to surrendered militants.

"You mean get co-opted like you? Yeah, I might," she said.

I THOUGHT I KNEW MY MA

I thought I could see my ma in a green and white polka dot frock sitting on her bed beside the window, looking out at the night sky, trying to capture the full moon between two pink wild roses blooming on the old creeper that curled itself around the bars of the window. I thought I could almost hear her sigh as she smiled to herself dreaming of a tall dark-haired man, clutching a microphone and singing in a gravelly voice on the Bihu stage, under another full moon. She thought that she would marry him when she grew up, and *koka* should have no opposition to that because although he was a Muslim, he was an artiste, and *koka* was an artiste, and he always said that literature and art should be the only two religions people were ever allowed to practise.

They were her religions too, although she also told *koka* that loving flowers should be another religion. She was practising her religion now, loving the flowers, letting them hold the moon in their bosom. The flowers shifted slightly in the breeze, and the moon was hidden for a moment. At that same moment, a shadow passed over her face. She was wishing he had not been a Muslim, because although art, literature and loving flowers should be the only religions, in Barbari where they lived, Hindu and Muslim were the only religions. The Muslims there were mostly immigrants, and *aita* said they fought over land and cut each other up at the slightest provocation and gave birth to lots and lots of children "so that they can grab some more of our land."

Of course, *aita* had eleven children, of whom my ma was the youngest. But she reasoned *koka* was very rich, and they could afford to have as many children as *aita* could bear. *Aita* was proud she could bear her husband so many children. *Koka*, of course, never knew how they were raised because *aita* kept them under her control and also, he was hardly ever home. If he was not supervising his vast land holding, he was settling some dispute in the village of which he was the undisputed patriarch because he had set it up by clearing the forests and settling people from his old village, and bringing Muslim agriculturists to work on their fields.

In the evenings, *koka* would be rehearsing for the next play the Rangmahal club would stage – he was their chief patron and often, the lead actor. When there was no play, Choudhury *koka*, Sirajuddin *koka*, Dambaru *mama* and everybody else would get together and discuss poetry or music. Sometimes, if the artiste was not travelling with his troupe, he would come and sing in their *batghar* – which *koka* had transformed into a *natghar*, *aita* often complained.

When the sounds of the rehearsals reached the main house, and *aita* retreated into the kitchen, my ma would sneak away from her study table and run to the *batghar*. It was through these rehearsals that ma had become close to *koka*, who liked that one of his children at least was interested in the arts. And *koka* forever for her remained the artiste, the lover of literature, and the man who always quoted Chandraprasad: *Xundarar Aradhanai Jibanar Khel:* the sport of life is in the worship of the Beautiful. Sometimes, the image of the Beautiful conjured up in her mind would be that of her father, sometimes of the artiste. She only ever wanted to be the silent worshipper.

I thought I could sense my ma's bewilderment when she was forced to come and live in Guwahati. I thought I could measure her reluctance. She had not wanted to come, but *koka* had insisted she get a better education than he ever did: "Study English literature, because it will teach you to appreciate how beautiful life is." She had heard from him that pain could be beautiful, and after the death of the artiste – some said from drinking too much, but she never believed them – she had often felt loss could be as precious as love. Without anybody knowing it, she had stolen the teacup kept aside for him – *aita* insisted that no Muslim could drink from the same cup as they did – and hidden it in her trunk under her bed. Although she hardly ever took it out of there, she liked to think: "this is the cup that 'runneth over' with my grief". She left behind the cup when she went to Guwahati and once when she came home for the holidays, she did not notice that it was gone from her trunk.

Just like the artiste's cup, many things had slowly slipped away from her unnoticed, but not her shyness, her solitude, and her love of the Beautiful, reinforced now by the English Romantic poets.

* * *

The silken slender threads of a mournful flute found her one day at her hostel window when she was once again toying with the moon. They were floating in from the direction of the boys' hostel, and she was immediately in love once again. Her artiste was back to life and she had found something to hold dear in this city where everything seemed daunting, everybody intimidating.

Majnixa xar pai xunisane ketiyaba ketekir hiya bhaga mat? She felt the bird's wailing that the poet heard in the middle of the night must have aroused the same pain, the same desire as the music of the flute now did in her. Sometimes she wondered who it was that could weave such sorrowful magic; often she told herself the magic was enough, the magician incidental.

And she would not have known if he had not played the same melancholy notes on College Day, and as she sat there in the auditorium with her friends, she suddenly, for a moment, went back to her old bed at home and could smell the wild roses at her window. But she was grown up now, and knew she could not dream of getting married to somebody just because they pierced your heart with so much pain. Because she knew now what marriage entailed and she could foretell how *aita* and *koka* would both react if they only knew she was in love with a tribal boy. *Koka* would perhaps understand the love and devotion, but she knew well enough now that abstract religions of the heart had nothing to do with the institutional religions people practised in everyday life, and even *koka* would not accept such a social ignominy as his daughter marrying a tribal boy. Oh, the tribals are Hindus alright, but they do still eat pork and drink alcohol. And although her elder brothers often went hunting in the reserved forest nearby and brought home deer meat almost every time, and maybe even ate wild pigs and buffaloes on the sly, pork – and of course beef – were taboo at home. And all the men of the house, including *koka,* only drank alcohol in secret, never socially like the tribals did. She had been shocked the day she found a bottle of rum in her father's safe which he had accidentally left open. She had never told anybody about it, and had later accepted that although drinking alcohol was bad, it is a weakness even the strongest of men must sometimes give in to. And then, they do say that artistes need alcohol. Was he drunk now?

Suddenly she came back to herself and realised she was sitting in the auditorium surrounded by an applauding audience, and blushed. The performance had ended, and she wished she could look at him for a little longer. Since she could not do that now, she started sitting towards the end of the classroom and watching shyly, guiltily, his profile on the boys' side of the room. And waiting for the evenings when she could listen to him playing the flute. She made believe that he played only for her, because she listened.

One day though, instead of the music, she heard a huge commotion from the direction of the boys' hostel. Some of the more adventurous girls in the hostel went over to the warden and brought back the news that the tribal boys had started a rebellion of sorts. They would no longer eat in the Second Dining Hall, they wanted to eat with the upper caste Hindu boys in the First Dining Hall. There was a little violence, and some of the boys on both sides had been injured. From the next day, she did not hear him playing the flute anymore. News was some of the boys in the hostel had been rusticated for indiscipline, he was one of them. Some of the other girls who had taken to openly declaring their adoration of him ever since College Day, proudly proclaimed that at least his sacrifice had set in motion a change that would be good for society. She wanted to cry because she hated it when they spoke about him as though he could ever belong to anybody but her.

* * *

I thought I felt my ma's trepidation the day she got married. I thought I knew how her tears were both of sorrow at leaving her parents' home and of fear of the unknown life she was about to start by marrying *deuta.* Her only consolation was that *koka* had himself chosen *deuta* to be her husband, and she knew he would never make a wrong choice for her. She had barely met him a few times before the wedding but she had read his novel and imagined he would be like Pramathes, the protagonist, who was a social activist and stood for all that was true, right and good. She was also a bit worried that if he was as good as Pramathes, she might not live up to his expectations.

But her sense of inadequacy began to disappear as she started learning a few lessons about life in the daily grind of marriage. The first of these lessons was that a man who was too good to be true should not get married. Unaware of his duties to his family, *deuta* indeed turned out to be like Pramathes, consumed with a desire for cleansing society of its evils and injustices. Perhaps it was something in the air in those days, but many other people like *deuta* also thought they could do this, and very naively they all joined the Axam Andolan – that massive civil unrest that turned our society upside down for nearly six years – a well-intentioned movement which a few self-serving people hijacked and turned into one that polarised our society, alienating all Muslims as well as tribals. People like my *deuta*, who had joined the movement because they wanted to fight for the rights of the "sons of the soil", did not realise this until it was too late. And then, when they did, they ended up as bitter defeated crusaders who remained, forever afterwards, cynical about any change in society.

Deuta could never get over it, and he changed, kept strictly to his textbooks and teachings, and pretty much banished whatever was left of Pramathes from his person. Meanwhile, my ma had already given up two of her favourite preoccupations, because early in the marriage, she had realised that it would not do for both partners to immerse themselves in art and literature, or there would be nobody to run the house, what with *deuta* also possessing, at the same time, an unbending social conscience. Since the same realisation had not come to *deuta*, it was my ma who had to relinquish her passion.

She did, however, keep her third religion alive, that of loving flowers. She had a huge garden with many different kinds of flowers to which she was more attached than to *deuta*. When I was born, she named me Pahi – flower petal – although she must have been disappointed that I did not turn out to be as delicate, as pliant, or as attached to her as her flowers. I was more attached to *deuta* who would sometimes, only for me, come out of his cynical shell and recount the fervour with which his generation had wanted to "save our nation and identity". Another generation was, at that moment in history, trying to do the same with guns and explosives and failing miserably, defeated by ideological poverty.

Growing up amidst all this and knowing what had gone before, I started believing that mass movements and armed insurgencies led nowhere. Revolution had to begin at the individual level, and I started my little rebellions. I began by renouncing the Brahminism I was born into. I took to eating beef and pork with friends, and later, travelling to places my mother would only have heard of, or my one-time social activist father would never have been acquainted with, where the people who he had once thought he was fighting for really lived. There, getting drunk on rice beer, we discussed ethnic reconciliation and religious tolerance, deliberated on blueprints of a future society without conflicts. And I thought I was in love with an indigenous Muslim boy who spoke with the same passion about the same things I believed in.

I thought my ma would be my worst enemy at this juncture. I thought *deuta* was the one who would understand. But it was *deuta* who very subtly blackmailed me into agreeing to marry Bordoloi *khura*'s son who lives in Bangalore. He stopped eating, and sat on his easy chair in the veranda for hours with a wounded look, the book on his lap open at the same page for a week. I gave in, but not before I realised my mother was on my side.

She said nothing the day I broke the news, and I would have thought she was silent only because *deuta* had said what she would have wanted to say, had she not come and sat beside me on my bed some days later and run her fingers through my hair. It was the day the love of my life had heaped accusations of hypocrisy and elitism on me and Bandini, seeing that I was well rid of him, came up to me and told me how he had been sleeping with another woman all along. My world and my rebellions and my beliefs had all come crashing down, but in the midst of it all, I suddenly saw my ma. I saw that my ma felt my pain, that she was indeed made of pain. And it was then, for the first time in my life, that I thought I should get to know her the way she must have been.

THIS IS HOW WE LIVED

It is nothing really. It is just the story of our lives, has been for years now, and we see no end to it. It is what happens to us – so many of us. It is just a kind of trade, routine at that. They buy us and they sell us, and because we want to live, we do not resist. We give in to their lust because most of the time, our lust for life proves to be more compelling. But sometimes, I feel that maybe it is not even really lust for them, you know. That maybe it is just an outlet, a way of getting it off their chests. Maybe if they did not rape us, they would fire at us instead.

They often do in any case, and indiscriminately too, like that Punjabi soldier from the nearby army camp did in our village five years ago and killed two children – brother and sister – walking home from school. The parents were later berated for letting their children walk around un-chaperoned while there was a war going on.

The army officer who had come to "pay his respects" to the family after the incident, ended up shouting, red-faced, at the wailing parents:

"*Kaise mata-pita ho?* What kind of parents are you, allowing your children to run around in the streets like this? Don't you know the terrorists are everywhere? We are here to protect you – but we cannot do our job properly if you do not cooperate! As it is, they killed your children see – the terrorists killed your children – it was their bullets that killed them. Do you understand? *Samjhe?*"

The PRO standing next to him was wincing visibly. So much for building personal relations with these people and trying to win them over and turn them against the rebels!

Although they did not understand much Hindi, in the face of the officer's tirade, the parents started wailing louder. What could they say that would convince anybody otherwise? Mangal and his gang – the village loafers who played carom all day under the *thinthlang* tree in the village square – had seen it all and had told them about the drunk soldier who did it before their very eyes. The soldiers would stop and play with them once in a while, during their patrols through the surrounding villages and chat with them, about games and sports and their families and friends back home. An uneasy camaraderie – if one could call it camaraderie – had developed between the two unlikely groups of people, one that would prove to have been illusory that day.

Like other days, that day also, the group of loafers had been playing carom when the patrol had come by. For some reason though, a few of the soldiers were drunk – one more so. He was in a completely inebriated state and had to be propped up by his colleagues every now and then. Even before they had stopped, he had started shouting obscenities at the boys, and not in the usual friendly manner. This had put Mangal and the others on alert, but even so, they were taken totally by surprise and were filled with fear when they saw him raise his gun and send a volley of mock fire all around him.

"*Jajajajajajajaja*", he had shouted in imitation of gunfire while turning round and round, taking aim at everything and everybody in sight, including his colleagues who watched him and laughed. After going at it for a while, he suddenly stopped. He had seen the two unfortunate children running down the street towards the square, the first ones to be rushing out of school at the end of the day as their mother had promised to cook special pork for them that day. And then, just as suddenly, the firing was not pretend anymore, but real. Real live bullets shot out of the gun and the two children dropped to the ground. The other children who were following them not very far behind, started screaming and running back to the school house. Mangal and his friends just stood there, petrified. The soldiers quickly got into action and rounded up their colleague and rushed away.

A few papers tried to report the truth, and people read the reports and were angry. But even though Mangal and one of our teachers spoke out, they could not get many other eye witness accounts to substantiate their claims. A few of the other newspapers, mostly the national newspapers that reported the incident in about 60 words because there were children involved, did not even bother to change the language of the press release handed out to them by the army PRO – that the boy and the girl had got caught in the crossfire during an encounter of the Indian Army personnel with "hardcore terrorists".

Our village stopped producing hardcore "terrorists" –

as they like to call them – after Simang died three years ago. Till then, we had really believed in the revolution, and thought it would do us good. Simang had been a very bright student from our school, and we all had great hopes of his going on to become the first graduate from our village. He had passed his matriculation from our school and had also finished his Higher Secondary studies from Barbari College in second class. Seeing that he had to walk 25 kilometers to the college every day, the teachers of our school had all raised money to buy him a bicycle. The day we handed it over to him, he had cried. We had told him we were giving it to him only on the condition that he would complete his studies and do something for the village and his people.

The headmaster's voice shook with emotion when he spoke to Simang from the dais during the function we organised to hand over the cycle to him: "You are our hope. This village, as much as this school, needs you to complete your education and come back and teach the younger generation the same values of community and culture that we inculcated in you. We are old now, our days are numbered. But you are the future. You will have to serve the cause of our people."

Simang did go on to serve the cause of our people all right, but not in the way we had thought. He joined the rebels while still in his first year of graduation studies, and we heard from him later that he had gone for arms training to many foreign countries. He was our local hero for many years thereafter, as were the six other young men, also like him, who had given up individual prospects to fight for the future of our community. For years afterwards, concepts like sovereignty and self-rule, identity and self-hood flooded our conversations and took over our minds. We were dazzled by the promise of a future where we would not be looked down upon, where we would be our own rulers, where we would have our own land, practice our own culture, enrich our own language, live lives of prosperity – in short, a golden future. And naturally, the young boys who were taking on the powerful Indian State in order to acquire that future for us, were our heroes.

It was only when the boys started dying and the army started their war on our hearts and minds and we saw no change in our sorry lots, that we began to see the futility of this golden dream. One by one, the boys from our area who had joined the rebels started to get killed, either in real or staged encounters. Simang's killing was staged to make it look like he had been trying to flee from custody, when the fact was that not only he, but his two brothers who were farmers, not rebels, had also been tortured to death. After this, nobody from our village joined the rebels. The loafers alone swaggered around posing as rebels and collecting money from people in the marketplace. "Protection money" they called it; they had finally found an occupation other than playing carom. The carom-playing had anyway stopped after the killing of the children.

In fact, after Simang and his brothers were killed, many things had changed in our village. The loafers, as I already said, became "self-employed"; the army started entering deeper and deeper into our community life, holding cultural shows in our villages and celebrating our festivals with us, and organising free health camps for our people, so much so that even if they killed our boys now, there would be some among us who would refuse to believe that those killed might have been innocent. And then, there was the complication posed by Mathuram's daughter.

Mathuram's daughter was picked up by a few soldiers one day, on her way to school – she was going to sit for her matriculation examination. She walked into a house full of mourners three days later, nothing Bodo about her except her looks. She was wearing a *salwar-kameez*, there was *sindoor* on her forehead and a *mangalsutra* dangled from her neck: her husband, a soldier from North India, was with her. They had been married by the priest at the small temple inside the army camp the day before. They sought the blessings of Mathuram and his wife, were granted it by the bewildered couple, and were gone two days later to the soldier's home in a small village in Uttar Pradesh. Even though marrying a *harsha* is a serious offence in our society and calls for a village council to levy fines and determine the offerings to be made to the gods, in this case, everybody was too fearful to attempt anything or show any contempt for the outsider.

Mathuram's daughter wrote regularly to her parents – I would read out her letters to them – about how happy she was in her new home, how her in-laws were so pleased that she was learning their language and customs so fast, and finally, in the latest one, how she was with the soldier's child. Her happiness confused us. It was easy to hate and fear the army as a whole for all the atrocities they committed, for all our people they killed, for standing in the way of our golden future. But then there was this one soldier from Uttar Pradesh, a *harsha*, who loved one of our girls so much, he married her and took her home where she was now expecting his child. Her letters told us everyday what a good man he was, how he brought so many presents for her every time he came back home from his distant postings. How now do we hate them all, now that we knew they were not all the same?

Already, the dream that we were given of a golden future had begun to be replaced by a banal reality of death and gore, the understanding that life would go on if we just started accepting everything passively, without complaint. When Simang and his brothers had been killed, we had taken out a silent protest march and tried to draw attention to such fake encounter killings. We also wanted to hire a bus and go to Dispur to hold a demonstration in front of the State Secretariat. But Simang's old parents stopped us.

"What good will it do? Our sons are not going to come back. Let the sons of the other people in the village live," they said.

That was our cue, and we started accepting whatever came our way with a kind of fatalism that was more ennui than stoicism. A few of our political leaders and human rights activists did stop by, but we were not the epicentre of the insurgent movement – ours was a small village, not in a Bodo majority area, surrounded by villages inhabited by innumerable other communities, and we had produced only seven rebels in nearly a decade. When they saw that we also lacked the will to fight back, they decided to leave us alone. In any case, there was no other major incident involving the armed forces or the insurgents in our village for a few years afterwards. Mathuram's daughter shook us out of our ennui for a while, but soon we learnt to live with that riddle as well.

That was when Bogi *bai* came to live in our village – when nothing seemed to have been happening at all, not even a skirmish, just a few local goons creating a fuss now and then. While everywhere in Assam bombs were exploding, planted either by the insurgents or by the security forces posing as insurgents; and people were being killed, arrested and maimed for crimes they had committed against the system as well as to cover up the crimes the system had committed against them; and politicians and activists were shouting hoarse about real or inflated injustices against our community, we just lived on from day to day.

She was the granddaughter of Shibram *daroga*, the only policeman our village had produced during the British Raj. When we were small, we would huddle around the *thinthlang* tree in the village square every evening and hear the stories our elders narrated about days past and places far away. One of their favourites was the story of Shibram *daroga*, the brightest boy in the entire village, who was orphaned at a young age. The day after his uncle, who had brought him up like his own son, got married to a young girl almost his age, he had decided to join the police force. Within a week, he had got married and left to join his new post in Guwahati. From there he took postings in Dhaka, Alipore, back to Guwahati, then Meerut, and so many other places, the names of which our elders could not even pronounce. They said he had once saved the life of a white man while he was posted in Dhaka, and that facilitated his quick promotion to the post of a *daroga*. In any case, as befitted a respected official of the British Raj, Shibram *daroga* never returned to his village in his lifetime, neither to meet his relatives nor to claim his ancestral land. Once in a while though, through messengers, he sent money to his aunt. The uncle had died a couple of years after the marriage leaving the young woman with a daughter and 10 *bighas* of land, half of which would have belonged to Shibram *daroga* if he had returned to claim it.

But he did not, and neither did his son, Pradip Musahary, who grew up and continued to live far away in Meerut where his father had built a house after retirement. He married a *harsha* from Himachal but she was not with him when he visited our village once, many years ago while I was still in college, to attend the wedding of his father's cousin's son. I remember how we stood and gawked at him from a distance and laughed as he awkwardly attempted to speak with his great aunt in Bodo. Finally, he gave up and spoke to her in broken Axamiya – Shibram *daroga* must have insisted on his speaking in Axamiya at home rather than in Bodo, because he thought that if his son ever had to return to Assam, he would have to speak the language of the majority. Tribal languages did not seem, at the time, to have any future in Assam and he had seen, as well as experienced, the disdain with which the Axamiya Hindus of the nearby village had treated the tribal people from his village. It was only after he became *daroga* and was posted in Guwahati once again, that he had been allowed into the houses of the Axamiya officers and aristocrats. On his first posting as a new recruit to the police force, fresh from the village, he had had to sit outside on people's verandahs and wash his teacup before leaving. He settled in Meerut because he did not want his only son to face this kind of treatment – at least this far away, nobody knew the difference between a Bodo and an Axamiya, and both were equally alien to them. And yet, Assam was home, and it was possible that he had hoped that someday, his son would return to the land of his ancestors. His son did not return, though, after that one visit. His granddaughter did. And she never left, till she died.

Bogi *bai* was not her real name, but we called her by that name because she was so fair, she glowed. Many people in the village initially thought she was a *daini* and wanted to kill her, or she would put a curse on our crops and on our children. It took a lot of effort on our part to dissuade them and to get them to believe she was only human. It took some more effort to get them to accept her presence in the village without complaint. And finally, after a year or so, almost none of us could remember a time when Bogi *bai* was not living in our village or was not a part of our everyday lives, strange though her ways had always been and continued to be.

She had only asked her cousins for one *katha* land – the rest, she said, they could continue cultivating as they had always done. Then, surprising us all, she built a mud and thatch house on her land – all the rich people in our village preferred to build concrete houses with cement and bricks, at times brought all the way from Guwahati. Then she began planting vegetables and fruits around the house in her small compound. Her cousins gave her a small amount of the paddy they produced and for the rest, she lived off her garden. Pulses, pork, chicken and fish were available in the *Bwjai* market every evening, but she almost never remembered to pick up her purchases from the market at the end of the day when she returned home. She would spend the afternoon and evening talking to the women who came to the market to sell silkworms and dried chicken skin, and all types of green leaves and vegetables, and pork and fish and *jou*. Almost every day, she would sit with the women in the *Bwjai* market and drink as much of the *jou* as the rest of them – sometimes more – and make them tell her all the stories of their lives.

"*De de*," the women would say to each other when they saw her drunk from the *jou*, "She is Bodo after all, although she talks like a *harsha*."

Bogi *bai* was only just picking up the language, and polishing it during her daily conversations with these women, and with the other people of the village.

Often, it would be late in the evening when she would walk back to her house, clutching a fat red diary where she would have made notes during the day, recorded anecdotes and entered little nuggets of information that she had picked up. She told us she was writing a book, a novel, for which she was living among us and talking to us about our lives – she visited every house in the village in the course of her first year, and always talked to everybody about their lives. Once, when she had come to the school to meet the teachers and speak to some of them, I asked her why she said so little about her own life.

"There is very little to tell, *abw*. I had a rich father, loving mother, comfortable upbringing, good education, and I lacked nothing; nothing except a sense of belonging. I did not belong even to my own husband after I got married. When we got divorced, I decided to come back and search for my roots. So here I am, although a little late in life, trying to understand who I am, where I came from. But I hope that at least, I can also tell the world a little bit of my story, our story, through my book, once I have actually grasped it myself."

This was the longest she had ever spoken about her "past life", as she jokingly called it many times, trying to evade the probing questions of the inquisitive villagers.

"Let us not talk about my past life, please," she would say. "I am here to talk about your lives, and write about you all."

And since they were flattered that they would be in a book that the whole world would read – it was to be written in English, and many of the villagers could not even write in Bodo – they would not pursue it any further, at least till the next time the occasion arose. After she told me about her divorce in school that day, I passed the word around that nobody should trouble her too much with questions about her past life since I sensed that it was not a very happy place for her. They had some regard for me – I was headmistress by now – and so they did not pursue the matter with her anymore, although they did pester me for details for a while. I had none, and had to cook up some, which I did, thinking and telling myself it was all for a good cause. I eventually managed to de-mystify her for the people of the village, although I wasn't any closer to solving her mystery for myself. Slowly, the questions subsided and Bogi *bai* became one of us and she remained so till she died.

Often, when she was returning home from her daily interviews, it would be dark. We all warned her not to walk back alone. After all, these were bad times, and even though we had created a bubble around us which no amount of mayhem could burst – or so we led ourselves to believe – we did know, deep down, that anything could happen at any time. There was the army camp just a few miles away from the village; there were the rebels who paid intermittent visits – to keep an eye on things; and most dangerously, there were the surrendered and pseudo rebels who knew nobody could touch them: they either had no scruples, in which case holding them accountable for their misdeeds would make no difference, or they were blessed by the state machinery and could thus not be held accountable for anything. True, we had taught ourselves to live with all of this or maybe, despite all of this. But it was also true that every once in a while, one of the households would find their daughter or wife or niece or mother gone for a night or two. And when they returned, they would be seen bathing themselves in the river over and over and over again. Everybody knew, but nobody wanted to say anything, because it was more important to go on living a lie than die facing the truth.

Ever since the army camp was set up in the nearby village fifteen years ago, every woman, every girl, for miles around knew instinctively to underplay her femininity, never to be out alone, especially after dark. Nobody thought of it as something unnatural; it had become a mundane part of our everyday life, this was how we lived. There was no point in attracting undue attention. They eventually spot you anyway, and summon you to the camp. But Bogi *bai* did not pay heed to our warnings. I sometimes suspected she must have felt that because she was educated and well off, and could speak Hindi in the same accent as the North Indian soldiers, she would never be manhandled by them. But all she said was,

"Who will harm me? If I am in any trouble on my way back, somebody will come to help me. Everybody in the village respects me, knows me."

Of course, nobody from our village would want to harm her but Gandrai was not from our village. He was from Kajalgaon, and he would sell his mother if they paid him two hundred rupees. Usually he got paid between fifty to a hundred rupees for the local girls, depending on how pretty they were or how drunk the soldiers were. But Bogi *bai* was a lady, extremely fair, and educated. She had to fetch a higher price.

So Gandrai sold Bogi *bai* to some soldiers from the camp and one night, they came and picked her up from her house. The next morning, some men from our village found her dead under the *thinthlang* tree, her *dakhana* lying on the ground near her. This was the first time any of our women had been killed. Usually they were kept for a night or two and then let go. But Bogi *bai* was dead. Maybe she had resisted; maybe the soldiers who bought her off

Gandrai were in a particularly bad mood. After all, they also have a hard life. Our boys who fight them know that we, their people, have to finally side with them no matter what – that is what community and kinship ties are for; but these soldiers do not even have the illusion of fighting for a cause. They face death every day for a pittance, to send home a few thousand rupees every month. Out of that, if they spent fifty or a hundred rupees on buying the bodies of our women, it does not perhaps seem like a bad bargain to them. It is perhaps like a routine trade, an outlet for their frustrations and the pressures of functioning under tough conditions in a conflict zone.

We do not want to be killed, and so we make these excuses for them. For ourselves, we say nothing, just wash ourselves ten times, maybe a hundred, and try to forget it happened, till it happens a second time perhaps, or a third. But if it happens even once, we get used to it, and inured to the ignominy. We have started looking at it less as an affront to our dignity and more as a price we have to pay for living in comparative peace in the midst of a mini war. We did not start the war, somebody else did. Many people are paying for it with their lives; the least we can do is be thankful we are alive. This time, however, it was different. This time somebody died; this time, Bogi *bai* died.

It seems she had had some influential friends in her past life, and when they got to know, they came to our village and did a spot survey and went back to Guwahati and submitted a citizens' report and demanded that an enquiry commission be set up. The newspapers also were full of the news for the next few days. The enquiry commission was set up within a month, and we heard every once in a while that there was some noise being created about the "case" either in Guwahati or Delhi, but both places were too far away from us. A couple of times, a few investigators came to question us if we knew who was behind "the incident". We all knew, of course, but nobody said anything because once the outsiders left, we would still have to live here. After some time, the investigators did leave and we heard nothing about the "case" anymore.

Bogi *bai* had been one of us. Her parents had died some time ago, and she had never mentioned any family left in Meerut. Nobody did, in any case, come forward to claim her; only her friends had come and they had done their bit, of course. But we were her family, her kin. So when her body came back from the autopsy, and they had taken as many samples as they needed to satisfy the press and the activists and the politicians and her influential friends that they were doing their best to identify the culprits, we did with her what we do to ourselves after coming back from the camp. We washed her body carefully, once, twice, three times, I don't know how many times, till we were sure that she was clean. And then, we cremated her.

NO GHOSTS IN THIS CITY

Growing up was living with a series of frights: of a snake in every hole on the cliff face, of landslide after every shower, of a ghost in every bamboo grove.

We lived in Guwahati city but high above it, in a house on the hill. It was a beautiful hill with nice people. The families were all closely knit at least in the beginning, and the extent of my entire world was up there – for the first 17 years of my life. And this world was haunted by the fear of many ghosts.

Almost everybody on our hill had seen a ghost. Das *khuri* once saw a cow floating a few feet above the ground. It was a black cow.

"Surely something bad is going to happen," she said.

And sure enough, *bar* Kakoti who lived in the road to Kharghuli died the next day.

"I told you something bad would happen!"

"But Kanak, he was 85 years old, it was high time he died in any case," her husband tried to reason with her.

"No, it is a sign," she insisted. "I must offer a *naibadya* and get the *aixakal*, the female worshippers to do a *nam*. *Krishna Krishna prabhu!* Some people can't stand other people's good fortune. This is black magic."

And then there was Labanya *baideu's pitha* stealing witch. Just before Bihu, everybody got busy making *pithas.* Every time you walked out of the house, you could hear the mortar and pestle in every house at war with each other, grinding rice. If you had the hand-held pestle, or *ural*, it was a nightmare – ma had too much to do already, so you would have to do the grinding. When your hands got tired, you exchanged with your brother the task of sifting the ground powder from the grain. Worse than this, however, was going to Labanya *baideu's* house and waiting your turn at the foot pestle, or *dheki.* She was the only one in the locality with a *dheki*, and everybody wanted to use it around Bihu. There was always a long line of people, and if you were lucky, about four back and forth trips of checking if the *dhekixal* was unengaged would ensure your turn at it. You had to be a shrewd calculator of how much time was left before the family ahead of you was done with their grinding. Ten minutes before they were done, you would have to stand guard at the *dhekixal* while your brother ran back and fetched ma or whichever of the grown-ups was available to work the *dheki.* Sometimes the competition was so tough that you did not get a chance for two or three days.

People stopped using Labanya *baideu's dheki*, though, after she reported that a *jakhini* had came to her house and stolen her *pitha.* They thought that she must be a witch too. Or that maybe she was keeping one as a pet. People with the power to tame a *jakhini* or a *bira* were not to be taken lightly, or crossed.

It was an old practice of the *jakhini* to stand outside the kitchen and steal *pitha* through cracks in the mud wall, while the housewife was baking them. *Aita* used to tell us about these *jakhinis* and how *aju aita* had actually caught one in the act; but I had thought witches usually stayed in villages and did not dare to come to the city. Even if they were in the city, they were supposed to confine themselves to the bamboo groves and thickets and come out of hiding in the afternoons, when there weren't too many people around – which is why ma would not let you leave the house on your own in the afternoons. But if the city witches had become so bold (or perhaps, so hungry) that they had started coming to people's kitchens at all odd hours, how could you be safe in your own house?

When on a short visit to the village, you could make sure you were never alone in the kitchen. But if the witches started visiting your house in the city, where you had to live every day of your life, even filling a glass of water for yourself could become a life-threatening exercise. What if the witch pounced on you? Sure you weren't baking *pitha*, but how would you know if the witch hadn't tasted something better and come back for it?

Randhoni aita was right when she said these supernatural folks were not to be trusted. She would not sleep alone in her room one night because the neighbour's son had died. Ma pointed out to her that she had a photograph of Krishna in her room. Didn't she believe in God enough to trust him to protect her from ghosts and spirits?

"Sure I believe in God," she said, "But I am not going to take any chances with this one. I had shouted at him quite a few times for stealing *kordoi* from our tree. What if he came and God took a long time to come out of the photograph? I would be dead, with nobody to account for it."

And then there was Akani *baideu*, who lived all alone in her brother's house because he thought it was not good enough for his wife. I always thought she was very brave, especially since it was a bit isolated and there was a neem tree below, and neem trees are supposed to be the dens of ghosts. But Akani *baideu* said she actually wanted to domesticate a *bira* and build him a tree house there. It would be fun, she said, to chat with him and learn magic tricks and other supernatural things from him. As it is, she said, she felt like a ghost herself, living alone in that house.

"So anybody who stays alone is like a ghost?!" I had asked her.

"No silly," she had laughed. "But it is easy to feel like one when you are alone."

I would be scared to feel like a ghost, I thought at the time, but it took me years to realise what she had really meant.

In any case, Akani *baideu* gave me the idea that ghosts always come solo. It was a consolation in a way that you would have to tackle only one ghost at a time, if at all. But when the *gamosa-pindha-bhoot* appeared in the bamboo grove, I was faced with the problem of how one would tackle half a ghost.

DSP Sarma reported seeing a ghost wearing a *gamosa* one night. He would have thought it was any man out for a stroll, but for the fact that there was only the *gamosa* and the two feet under. Waist upwards there was nothing, or nobody.

It could be, Brajen *dada* laughed, that his father had seen a real man, and in the darkness, only the white *gamosa* had registered with him. As it is, he had cataract in his eyes and loved writing stories for children. He had even managed to get a book published after his retirement from the police service. They said he had paid to get the book printed, but that is beside the point. The point is that DSP Sarma's ghost scared everybody so much that they would not come out of doors after dark for a long time. Only Brajen *dada*, Khanin *dada*, Haren *dada* and their gang had the courage to hold their regular *adda* still at the bench in the *kolorpar* field – and the bamboo grove was just off the field.

I refused to open my eyes every time we crossed that way after dark, and would hang on to any adult arm that was available at the moment. I did not let anybody know, of course, that that was how I walked across *kolorpar* every time but I did that for quite a few years, till Anjali came to live in our locality and suggested we go looking for the well where the ghost's body was supposed to have been dumped by the "Bangladeshis" who had killed him. The story was that during the *Axam Andolan*, some of the activists had been hiding in the jungle on our hill. One party had been discovered by militant immigrants and butchered. The remains had been thrown into a well that had since been covered by bushes. What I could not understand was that if the entire party was butchered, why did we see only one ghost? Or was it the collective ghost of the entire team? And was the *gamosa* a sign of their Axamiya nationalist sentiments?

I wondered, but I never had the courage to try and find the answers – till Anjali became my neighbour, and she was so overbearing and so disparaging, that I agreed to go with her in search of the well and see if the stories were true. By that time the ghost had become a permanent resident of the Chintachal hill and though not many people had actually seen him, his presence was taken for granted. I had also reconciled myself to the idea that since he had not harmed anybody so far, he would not harm me. Also, he was an Axamiya ghost and I fancied myself a die-hard Axamiya nationalist by then, wanting to join the insurgents to fight the glorious battle for a sovereign socialist Assam. I told myself that his generation had started the fight for Assam's dignity and rights and mine will take that fight forward. What kind of a revolutionary would I be if I was scared of a ghost, and that too a patriotic ghost?

So I went with Anjali on an excursion into the thickets and we found the well, but little else. There were no weapons lying around nor any tell-tale signs that a massacre had happened there.

"See, no signs. Therefore, no ghost," she declared sanctimoniously.

I did not see why there should not be a ghost just because we could not find the remains of the dead man/men, but I was not going to say that to Anjali. She was not a weakling who believed in ghosts, and I was not going to admit to her I was. She claimed to be a "grown-up mature adult woman" – those were her pet words – and I wanted to be like her. So I convinced myself that she was right, that ghosts did not exist, that it was childish to believe in them. I was also a grown-up mature adult woman and I would no longer believe in ghosts; they were all in the mind, and that was that. I started looking up and into the bamboo grove every time I passed that way, forcing myself to overcome my fear. And I did that every time for the next few months that we lived on the hill.

* * *

When we moved out of our house on the hill, my little perch on top of the world was irretrievably lost, and I found myself in the city below, the city I had shut out of my loft atop the hill. In this city, I did not have to try very hard to not feel afraid. I found that the ghosts of my childhood had quietly faded away. They could not stay in a city that I discovered had lost its soul and drowned in a cacophony of disinterested silences. Silences that saw but turned away from the real live ghosts of the land: people – just alive – who would have been better off as ghosts, and who are alive only because they could not all be killed. These were the ghosts of people who have seen other people live, love and laugh, and then get slaughtered in the name of ethnicity without ideology, by nationalists awaiting their turn at the cash counter, who, while the wait is on, find diversion in shooting off a few rounds of loud bullets and shouting a few nationalist slogans. I had not bargained for this. I had not thought the lights that twinkled when I looked down from my hill were there so the ghosts could lose their way. My childhood ghosts can definitely not live in this city, because if you are a ghost, you would want people to see you and to believe in you; and here in this city, nobody believes anymore.

VIRGINIA *MAHI*

Bortee *mama* and Xorutee *mama* were the twins and younger than Virginia *mahi.* Baganor *koka-aita* did not name their daughter Virginia. The Christian midwife did. The midwife was a tea-tribal woman who lived in the labour lines and picked tea leaves like all the other labour women. Her name was Rojina. Midwifery was Rojina's "side business" and they said there was no one who knew more about bringing babies into the world than she did. Even Bijon Roy Compounder who was the only medic in the tea estate, had had to take her help in many complicated pregnancies.

Anyway, Rojina brought Virginia *mahi* into the world and predicted that she would grow up to be a very beautiful woman. "Like the Virgin Mary," she said and Virginia she named the baby.

Baganor *aita* always had a tough time with babies. Had Rojina not been there, everybody says, neither *aita* nor Virginia *mahi* would have made it. As it happened, Virginia *mahi* came into the world safe and healthy, and as Rojina had predicted, she grew up to be quite a beauty.

Baganor *aita* however, was not very healthy after

Virginia *mahi*'s birth. She had always been a frail woman, and when a few years later, Xorutee and Bortee *mama* were to be born, everybody thought she would die. But again Rojina took charge of things and the twins were born, and Baganor *aita* did not die. But then, she never really recovered either. She continued to be weak and fell ill so often that nobody was really sad when she died.

"It's a mercy on her," they said.

But I suppose it was a mercy on the entire family, especially on Virginia *mahi*, who had always had to look after her mother instead of her mother looking after her. Our own *aita* said that in their family, the roles of mother and daughter were quite reversed.

When Baganor *aita* died, *koka*, who loved her very much, took a transfer and went off to work in a tea company in Upper Assam. Virginia *mahi* and the twins stayed back and *koka* said, "My Virgie is such a capable and responsible girl, she can look after her brothers while I'm away."

So Virginia *mahi* looked after her brothers, and when Baganor *koka* came home on his monthly visits, she looked after him as well.

Only, in the process, she forgot to look after herself. So one month when Baganor *koka* came home, he realised Virginia *mahi* was pregnant. And she was only sixteen. Baganor *koka* felt he could not carry the burden of the shame on his own, and he dragged Virginia *mahi* to our *koka-aita*'s house and handed her over to our *aita*. *Aita* sent for Rojina who also knew more than others about *not* bringing babies into the world.

After a month, Virginia *mahi* went back to her own

home, and Baganor *koka* also came back home for good. And when we went visiting next, it was like old times again. Baganor *koka* gave us rides on his bicycle through the tea garden. He did not mind when we put our hands into the pockets of his shorts looking for lozenges. He said he was younger than our *koka* and so, he wore shorts instead of *dhutis* like our *koka* wore. We did not believe him, of course, because our *koka* looked so much younger and was so much more active even though he wore *dhutis.*

Then Virginia *mahi* gave us orange cream biscuits, and when we pestered her, she also made *malpuas* for us. In the evenings, she sat down with us and told us stories.

Bortee *mama* was always studying, but he would not mind taking some time off to ask us about our studies. Xorutee *mama* was hardly ever there. We always went hoping he would be, though, because when he was there, he would teach us how to climb trees, pluck fruits for us, and tell us about the leopard he and his friends saw among the tea bushes at night when they went there for a picnic. At this, Baganor *koka* would tell him to shut up and not frighten us kids, and Xorutee *mama* would shut up and walk into his room, and not come out for the rest of the time that we were there. That is why, we never wanted Baganor *koka* and Xorutee *mama* to be home at the same time. They seemed to be fighting all the time.

One day, we heard Xorutee *mama* had left home after a fight with Baganor *koka.* They tried to trace him, but he was nowhere to be found. Our visits to Virginia *mahi* stopped. Our *aita* said we were not to trouble her and Baganor *koka* as they were very sad. We thought we could cheer them up if we went, but *aita* still would not let us go. Instead, we were sent back home to Guwahati.

Guwahati was a different place altogether, with different people and different sets of growing-up problems. And after a while, we quite forgot about Virginia *mahi* and Xorutee and Bortee *mama* and Baganor *koka*.

Then suddenly, one day, Virginia *mahi* turned up at our place in Guwahati. There was a girl with her whom we had never seen before. *Mahi* said she was Xorutee *mama*'s wife, and could she stay with us for a couple of days till she caught her train back to Calcutta?

"Calcutta?" my ma asked.

"Yes," she replied, and explained that Xorutee *mama*'s wife was from Calcutta. A year after he had left home, Xorutee *mama* had sent word that he was in Calcutta and doing well. He would not be coming back home again. But he had to come back four days ago to attend Bortee *mama*'s *shraddha*.

After we had left Kopati, Bortee *mama* had joined the *xangathan*. He had given up his studies to become a revolutionary. And last week, he had been picked up by the army. They had beaten him to death. Virginia *mahi* cried when she told us she had gone to collect the body, but could not make out at first which one was Bortee *mama*'s. When they had picked him up to place him on the pyre, his head had rolled back on his neck – there was not a single bone intact in his body.

Baganor *koka* had taken to bed as soon as he heard of Bortee *mama*'s death. And when Xorutee *mama* had come home, he had been taken to the army camp too, for questioning. He had not come back since, and Virginia *mahi* had decided it would be best for his wife to go back to Calcutta and wait for news there.

"And what about you, Virgie?" my ma asked.

"I am going back home to look after *deuta*," she said, and left.

SIN AND RETRIBUTION

I froze in the middle of a carefully calibrated stroke of my *da.* Somebody was shouting,

"*Oi* run, run! CRP!"

Maybe it was Ramen.

But how could it be? How could the reserve police be there already? Not even half of Nayagram had been covered yet, and it was a small village, just a cluster of 20 huts or so.

"*Ha Hari! Pala, pala!* Who informed them?"

I could make out it was Pulakes's voice not very far from me.

"Must be Ratan. *Salla,* son-of-a-pig humanist!" I wheezed.

It is no easy task cutting up live human beings. And these were strong hardy peasants; and their multiple wives and the plentiful children that they produced.

"Imagine," Saikia *saar* had told us last week at headquarters, "Here is a village of 20 families, but with a population of 200! They breed like animals and take from us what is ours by right."

He told us they had grown strong because we let them.

We allowed them for so many years to be bred, fed and made strong on food that should have been ours, cultivating land that was ours, usurping our livelihood and threatening our identity, growing stronger and proliferating every day.

No, it was not an easy task at all.

It had not been an easy task planning the attack either. We had to catch them unawares, unarmed. We had been told these peasants were dangerous when their meagre possessions were threatened, and very obstinate about clinging on to their pathetic lives. We had also been warned not to underestimate them – they were survivors who had lived through famines and floods, military oppression and brutal massacres. They had come here determined to survive, but if we wanted to put an end to their silent invasion, we would have to exterminate them. We should however never, ever consider their docility to be their weakness.

Thus it was that we had planned the attack for tonight. It was *eid*, and the whole day, the people of Nayagram had been feasting. At least, the few who had stayed behind – around 70; the rest had gone back to their old villages for the festivities.

Nayagram was a newly set up village, the land had only just been reclaimed five years back by Bordoloi *mohori* of our Na Pam village, and in that time, he had encouraged these filthy peasants also to come and settle. They were, after all, cheap labour for the vast stretches of land that he had claimed for his own – it helped to be a government appointed land revenue official. He had had to give a few *bighas* of land to the *matabbar* of the immigrants, Kasem

Ali, to persuade him to resettle the peasants from their old villages, but that was a small price to pay. Kasem Ali must have had very little problem convincing these twenty families to move. Always starving, relentlessly breeding, they are anyway forever on the lookout for newer areas to encroach.

"Before long, we will no longer be Axamiya. We will all be *Miya*, all Muslims. Our names will have Ali or Begum attached to them, and we will be speaking their filthy tongue. Our long suffering Axami *ai*, our dear land, will be swallowed whole by these land-hungry invaders. We will soon be part of Bangladesh. Is that what you want?"

Saikia *saar*'s words had been ringing in my years since last week, and killing these usurpers had seemed like the only way to save our motherland and our national identity. The others also must have been thinking along the same lines, but it was not until Pulakes blurted out loud "Let's kill those bastards, *kela*!" that the rest of us admitted we were thinking the same. Saikia *saar* had just left after our afternoon tea session. In the short time that we had set up our village level branch of the Assam Nationalist Youth League, we had begun to refer to the tiny one-room structure we had erected with bamboo cut down from Bordoloi *mohori's* backyard as headquarters.

Saikia *saar* had walked into headquarters one afternoon a couple of years back to have tea with us while we were racking our brains about what to do next, having played ten games of carom since the morning and endless rounds of cards. He was the headmaster of the Dhaniram Saikia Secondary School built in memory of his late father in the nearby Purani Pam village, as well as the headman of the same village. Always dressed in a pristine white *dhuti* and cotton shirts stitched from hand woven cloth, he had a reputation of being the most learned man in Purani Pam and everybody revered him. Even Bordoloi *mohori* who was the richest man in the area could not take any decision without at least informing Saikia *saar*. It was with Saikia *saar's* blessing that he had resettled almost his entire clan and scores of people besides from the neighbouring villages in his native Nalbari district near Purani Pam village. That is how our village of Na Pam had come up a decade or so ago. Slowly, the *mohori* had begun to reclaim more and more land around the village so that Nayagram had to come up next. Since Purani Pam was the name of the original village in the area, the later villages that grew up around it came to have the prefixes 'Na' and 'Naya', respectively the Axamiya and Bengali words for 'new'.

We got to know all this from Saikia *saar*. He was a repository of knowledge and as his visits to our headquarters became more and more frequent, we came to look at him more and more as our advisor and guide, our ideologue. He told us that he was not too happy about bringing the immigrants to our area, but Bordoloi *mohori* had been adamant.

"What could I do? He is the richest man, I am a simple teacher."

Saikia *saar* was such a humble man! We knew he was quite well to do and owned a lot of land himself, although of course, Bordoloi *mohori* owned much much more. Nobody however, could have been richer in experience and knowledge than Saikia *saar*. But he never had any airs about him; he was always soft spoken, unassuming, and as time went by we realised how much he was influencing us for the better. He not only instilled in us a pride of being Axamiya but also made us realise the importance of self-help.

He said we Axamiya people had always been laid-back, and so the British could come and enslave us. After the British left, it was now the Muslims who were occupying our land and usurping our livelihood. Our forefathers had never allowed the Muslim rulers to occupy our land but now, we were giving in to these lowly peasants without a fight. We were too unconcerned about our own welfare to protest. Meanwhile the Indian government showed a step-motherly attitude towards us and turned a blind eye to our woes. What Saikia *saar* told us was of course nothing new – we had been reading about all this in newspapers and our nationalist magazines for a few years now. All over Assam, there was a growing wave of resentment against the Muslim invaders. We also heard of isolated incidents here and there where protests had taken place urging the government to take steps to safeguard our land and identity and oust the immigrants. At places, these protests had also turned violent. What Saikia *saar* did was to make us realise that these were not incidents that we could afford to just read about and forget. If people all over the state were rising in protest, we should also do our bit. We were also, after all, not unaffected by the rampant immigration.

"Look at our own village," he reminded us. "We were two Axamiya clusters living peacefully – the old and the new, Purani Pam and Na Pam – and then came the Muslims and set up a 'Nayagram'. Why should we allow them to enter our midst, I ask you? Before long, you will see them multiplying by hundreds, taking over our economy, vitiating our language. Our boys will soon take to eating beef and we will all be forced to turn Muslim. Is that what you want? It is a good thing that you have taken the initiative of starting this village level branch of the League. You are bright boys, you are our future. You will have to lead the resistance in our village. We are old people, worthless. Our days are over. But you will have to preserve the Axamiya identity for *your* progeny."

Finally, we had a sense of purpose. Finally, we realised that we could do something about the sorry plight of our motherland, make our lives worthwhile. Everywhere in Assam, we kept hearing now about so many martyrs killed while confronting immigrants. The Indian armed forces and the central reserve police forces were all in league with these immigrants, always safeguarding them. So many of our Axamiya boys fell prey to their bullets and batons. Only in our village, we were doing nothing. We were still silent.

Then last week, after Pulakes spoke our minds, we decided it was time for action. Just a few days ago, an entire village of immigrants had been massacred by 'unknown assailants' in our adjoining district. Everybody had been horrified, but not many had shown much sympathy for the immigrants.

"They will breed back again," everyone said.

It was easy to come to terms with these incidents if

we did not think of those killed as human beings, and that was what everybody did. We also did the same thing while we made our frenzied plans for the day of *eid.* We hardly had five days' time between Pulakes's outburst and *eid*, the day when we knew we could safely attack. There would be very few people in the village and all of them would be tired from the festivities. Despite the incidents elsewhere in Assam, the Nayagram immigrants were not expecting any violence to break out in their village. After all, they had the patronage of the richest man in the area, and despite the threat posed by the League members in major immigrant inhabited districts of Assam, our village level branch had never been quite so active. Though I am not proud of it, I guess we were seen as a bunch of unemployed idlers who had started the branch for want of anything better to do. Even my own father, with whom I speak less and less every day, complains incessantly about how I waste my days with the other loafers, playing cards and carom and running up a huge tab at Bhola's tea stall.

"But that will act to our advantage, don't you see?" Ramen had said. "The element of surprise is essential in such enterprises. Nobody will expect us to take matters into our own hands in this way, and so nobody will suspect our involvement in it as well."

Ramen fancied himself well read in literature about guerilla tactics. He had borrowed a Mao Tse Tung book from his brother, Ratan, when we started planning, and flipped through its pages. Ratan had asked a lot of questions when he saw his good-for-nothing younger brother sitting with the book in the old armchair on the veranda. Ramen assured us he had allayed his brother's suspicions tactfully, but we were all a little uneasy after that.

And now, Ratan must have informed the CRP company posted in the adjoining district. How he knew about our plans was beyond us, but then Ramen was not the brightest star in our group. He must have let something slip. As it is we had not been able to cover much ground – it is not easy, like I found out, to slaughter a human being. A goat or a chicken is different – it does not wail in your language while being butchered. We had not foreseen this. I almost lost my nerve a few times and once, felt quite frightened when I saw a group of people emerge from their huts at the far end of the village. But they were only trying to make a run for it and probably went and hid themselves in the jungle nearby. I had pushed on. And now this!

Pratap had assured us that he had had a word with OC Hiren Kalita, who had recently been transferred to our police station. He said the officer had assured him he would not interfere.

"Just signal when you are done, I will bring my men. I have to be seen as doing something, *nohoine*? Heh, heh!"

After all Kalita was also Axamiya, and hated the immigrants as much as we did. But the CRP? Where did they come from? They were camping a few villages away; Ratan must have informed them well in time if they were already here.

There was nothing to be done now but flee. We all ran. We made our way through the dead bodies and jumped over other bodies that would probably have been better off dead, and ran. We scattered in different directions as we had already planned to do after our task was complete. Even as I ran, I thought I saw Ramen picking up something from among the dead bodies. I could not stop to find out what. Then my red Naga shawl got stuck as I turned in the direction of Na Pam. I bent down to release it by brushing away what could have been a small hand or a fallen branch. I did not have time to think about it. I also heard police sirens. Naturally, Kalita could not be caught doing nothing when the CRP arrived.

I crossed the bamboo thickets praying that I would not trip and fall, or worse, get bitten by a sleeping snake on whose tail I might inadvertently step. When I was clear of it, I made for the first house I saw. It was Sharma *saar*'s. He had been our Axamiya teacher in college, and we had always made fun of him in class. At least till we realised that he had just moved to our village. My father would have skinned me alive if *saar* had ever complained about my behavior in class. After that, we confined ourselves to deflating the tires in his bicycle so that he would have to pull it along the entire five-kilometre stretch home.

I knew *saar* was the nervous kind. We had often made fun of the way he looked so alarmed every time somebody so much as said "*namaskar saar*" to him outside class. Only while delivering his lecture inside the classroom did he ever exude any confidence. At other times, he would jump at everything. I knew that if I knocked on his door now, he might have a heart attack. But I had no option, the sirens were drawing nearer. I prayed that *baideu*, at least, would have the courage to come to the door. She had taught us history and was rather stern, quite unlike her husband. We all used to be afraid of her in college.

I wiped my face as clean as I could on my shawl, hid the *da* under it, and made my way as quietly as I could to the kitchen door at the back. I winced as I stepped on the *kharikajai* planted along the drawing room wall just below the window. *Baideu* would definitely not like it when she saw the plight of her plants in the morning. But I had no way of avoiding them as I groped my way along the side walls of the house in the near complete darkness.

Our League had called for a black-out that day in the entire state as a protest against the state government's inability to throw out the immigrants, and the central government's apathetic stand towards the entire issue. Everybody was bound to follow our diktat or their houses would be stoned and windows broken. We had imposed the last few calls successfully and I was glad to see that nobody in Na Pam dared leave their lights on anymore during blackouts.

There was only a faint yellow glow visible along the outline of the kitchen window that had newspapers pasted on the panes. As I had hoped, *saar* and *baideu* had not gone to bed yet. Nobody did sleep very well these days. I imagined they must be sitting at the kitchen table keeping vigil. And then of course, the sirens were also sounding quite loud by now. As I approached the kitchen door, I could hear soft murmurs. I knocked softly on the door. The murmurs suddenly died out, the yellow glow faded.

"*Saar, baideu,* it's me – Prabin. Can you please open the door?"

When I heard no movement inside, I knocked again, a little louder. This time, *baideu* opened the door a crack. *Saar* stood behind her. I could sense rather than see the fear on her face, and although in the near darkness I could not see his, I imagined it would be contorted in terror.

"*Bopa*, what are you doing here at this time? And what is all this commotion about? What is happening?"

"There was a raid at our League office. Somebody misinformed the police that we were hiding arms there. Can I come in and stay here for the night till this is over?"

I could sense them stiffen, and I knew that they did not believe a word of what I had just said. With his hand clutching the kitchen door for support, Sharma *saar* was visibly shaking, so was the door itself. But *baideu* was a sensible woman. She knew it would be no good trying to turn me away. I blessed my quick thinking about the arms story. Now even if they did not believe my story, they would not dare raise an alarm.

Baideu let me in and quickly shut the door again. The sounds of the sirens faded. I felt safe in the glow of the dimmed oil lamp. As I stood in the middle of the kitchen floor now, unsure of what to do next, there was an uneasy silence for a short while. *Baideu* broke it.

"You will eat something?" she asked rather stiffly.

"No, *baideu*."

"You will sleep?" she asked again.

"If you can spare a room..."

She said I could sleep in the drawing room. Their two children, Majoni and Moina, were asleep in the other room and she did not want them woken up.

"That will do fine. I can sleep on the drawing room floor. I will leave before Majoni and Moina are up. No need to see me out in the morning. I will leave before dawn." I knew I was rambling. A combination of relief at finding someplace to hide and rest for the night, and tiredness from the night's labour was catching up. I fell asleep immediately, as soon as I lay down on the drawing room carpet.

I do not think *saar* and *baideu* slept that night. I could not be sure. I was woken up by *baideu's* screams.

"Moina, Majoni! Don't touch that!"

It was light outside. I had overslept. I sat up quickly. I saw that Moina was holding my *da* in his hands, Majoni was picking at the dried blood on it with her tiny fingers. The Naga shawl I had used to wrap the *da* in lay at their feet, thick with dried blood. *Saar* stood in the doorway afraid to come in. And *baideu* was pushing him out of her way, screaming and lunging at the children and finally, snatching the *da* from them. She then ran at me with it, brandishing it menacingly.

"You dare come into my house with blood all over you. You dare teach my children your murderous ideology. Murderer!"

Last night in the darkness, they must not have seen anything, but now that it was daybreak, I imagined they could probably see my hair matted with blood, my clothes caked with it. The children however did not seem perturbed. Moina's bright eyes were turned towards me in fascination; and Majoni was now picking the blood stuck in her fingernails with rapt attention.

"Labhita, don't! Let him go. He will go away. Go *bopa*,

go, please leave. We will not tell anyone you were here. Just don't come back. Please!"

Sharma *saar* seemed to have finally found his voice. But he pleaded with me from the doorway, and still did not enter the room. A few steps from me, *baideu* suddenly broke down. She crumpled on to the floor and began to weep and wail.

Saar was still trembling and *baideu* still on the floor when I packed the *da* once again in my shawl and left. And I was shivering violently when I drowned both shawl and *da* in the river on my way home. I figured I could not go home looking like this and took a quick dip in the river myself and saw the water around me turn red.

* * *

We met at headquarters that evening. All of us looked like we had slept through the day. At least, I knew I had. At first we could not think of anything to say to each other. Then Pratap said,

"At least we are all safe."

"Yes," we all murmured.

"It was close though," Pulakes began.

"I will deal with Ratan, *salla*, just wait!" said Ramen. "Thank god, it was not an utter waste."

Then he emptied his pockets out. He placed a few bangles and finger rings and earrings, gold and silver, on the table. I jumped. One earring still had the lobe attached to it.

THE SWING

There was a *jalpai* tree in the backyard of Ajoli *pehi's* house, and there was a swing hanging from the *jalpai* tree. At least, I suppose you can call it a swing. Actually it was a loop of thick rope with its two ends tied to the sturdiest branch of the tree. Whenever we were in the village and wanted to sit on it, we had to carry our own cushion from the sofa set in the drawing room and put it back when we were done. *Pehi* would be very angry if any of us forgot. But if Aimoni left her cushion behind, *pehi* would not say anything. She would pick it up herself from wherever in the vicinity of the tree Aimoni would have flung it, and take it back inside the house.

It was Aimoni's swing and she had been swinging on it for the past eighteen years. *Peha* had fixed it for her when she was five years old and after he was killed, she took to sitting on the swing every single day for the rest of her life. She always had a toothy smile plastered on her face no matter what, but as the people in the village whispered to one another, *"She must still remember the horror!"*

It was not as though Aimoni did not like us using her swing. We just tried not to be around when it was time for her to come out and sit on it. She always went there around noon – in summer then, she sat out the hottest part of the day on the swing. It suited us well since *we* did not want to be out in the hot sun. We were a little jealous in winter though, because then she got to soak in the warm sun. But she did not even change her routine when it was raining. We often heard *pehi* cry in front of ma: "What good will it do to her to have the physical strength of an ox? What if she is built to resist every illness? If only her mind could function..."

Once during one summer vacation when we were visiting, I was still on the swing reading a book when Aimoni turned up at her usual time with her cushion clutched to her chest – she had her own cushion and did not have to pick hers up from the drawing room. I knew I had trespassed when I saw her standing there smiling her toothy smile, but with tears rolling down her cheeks. I left immediately.

Of course we had not always been so indulgent towards Aimoni when it came to the swing. There had been innumerable fights between us and *pehi* regarding the swing.

"Why can't we sit on it when we want? Why should Aimoni be allowed to sit on it whenever she wants, and not us? Does it have her name written on it? No, it does not!"

Pehi of course was not known for her patience and she shouted back at us calling us all kinds of names: *jahanit jawa, mannei mara*: and she always cursed us at the top of her voice: "*Tonthor potan hobo*!"

Then when her stock of choice abuses was exhausted, she would sit down on the ground and start wailing:

"What have I done to deserve this? Whose drinking water have I poisoned? Why should this happen to me? Nobody understands how I am making ends meet – slaving day in and day out to feed and clothe myself and this worthless creature. He who had to leave has left – he has left me in the middle of this vast ocean to fend for myself and his daughter. Why did he not take her with him? She is better off dead anyway..."

And so on and so forth. And Aimoni always won because we could not take *pehi's* outbursts for too long, and would give up trying to appropriate the pleasures of the swing.

"Who wants to sit on the swing anyway?" we would say as kids. "We do not want to be infected by sitting on the same swing as a dumb mad girl."

It was only much later that we learnt how cruel these words were. Ma heard us calling Aimoni 'mad' one day and she called us aside and explained to us that she was not really mad. She just had not grown up. And as grown-ups ourselves, it was our duty to indulge our younger ones. We were then at a stage when we wanted to appear heroic to ourselves, and we were easily swayed by ma's reasoning. Let Aimoni have her swing – she had nothing else. Besides, we had it to ourselves during the more pleasant parts of the day.

The truth about *peha*, *pehi* and Aimoni, and the 'horror' that the villagers all talked about, was much longer in coming to us. By then, one by one, we had grown out of the swing, out of childhood and adolescence; our visits to the village also became fewer as we ventured out of the protective circle of our families to try our luck in the wide world outside. Only Aimoni had remained where she was, the way that she was. She never outgrew the swing. She still carried her now-tattered cushion – with countless multicolored patches stitched on to it by *pehi* – out to the backyard every day. She still sat on the swing, and holding on tightly to the rope on one side, swung gently to and fro, backwards and forwards. Sometimes, she would experimentally lift her feet off the ground a couple of inches. Then a couple of more inches. If you were watching her from the guest room window, you could see her stiffen. Then she would give a jerk to the rope with her bottom. Nothing. Another jerk, this time more vigorous, and the swing would move to and fro, the wrong way sideways. That was the only time you could see something in her eyes other than a vacant stare if you were watching her surreptitiously, as I often did. You could see naked terror. Aimoni anyway had large round eyes that would now open wider still, and she would clutch on to the rope tighter with both hands. She would involuntarily lift her feet higher and try to pull them closer to her body. There would be some more moments of terror on the wildly swaying rope after this, before it would occur to her to drop her feet back to the ground. Then, when she was steady once more, she would sit stone still on the swing, not moving a muscle. First, her body would relax little by little; then, she would start swinging again. To and fro. Backwards and forwards. Heel to toe. Gently, gently. And gradually, the look of terror would drain away from her eyes, slowly, ever so slowly.

Was this same look there in her eyes the day she and her mother watched as her father was trampled to death by heavy military boots, and the bones of his body broken by the repeated assault of heavy AK-47 rifles? She would have been too young to understand what was going on – just a little over five years of age. But *pehi* had seen it all. Was that why she was so bitter? I often used to wonder why she kept saying Aimoni was better off dead, and for most of my adolescent life, secretly hated her for that.

Aimoni had by then become the heroine of many of my experimental short stories (that read more like romantic tales actually), each having a different set of nasty and nice characters who tried to molest or seduce her. In these tales, I was the protective elder brother who would save her from the sex crazy wolves in sheeps' clothing and give her hand away in marriage to an earnest young man who would swear eternal love to her despite her 'condition'; and they would live happily ever after.

Such romanticism flew out of the window when I was confronted with the truth. The brutality of real life haunted me forever afterwards when I came to know about the horrors *pehi* had witnessed that one night during Operation Bajrang when the army came to the village looking for insurgents and instead, killed anybody who resisted entry into their houses. Everybody in the village had heard about the rape of young women in neighbouring areas by the army men, and *peha* had only wanted to protect his wife and daughter from the men pounding on his door and shouting at the top of their voices for him to open the door, or else. His little daughter had woken up amidst the din and was now crying, demanding to be held in her father's arms. When they had finally broken down the door, they had flung the little girl from the father's arms and she had landed against the wall at the far end of the room. Was it then that Aimoni had lost her speech and damaged her brain? Or was it later, when she had sat on the floor watching her father beaten to death and her mother holding on to the feet of one of the army *jawans* pleading with them to spare her husband? There was no rape in the village that night – Aimoni's father had misjudged the army men who had come to their village. But then he did not live through the night to realise his mistake. And although his wife and daughter lived, one was better off dead and the other continued to complain that she was not.

Grown-ups tend to avoid talking about such horrors in front of children for fear of traumatising them, and our parents, aunts and uncles all tried to spare us the truth for so long. They did not realise, however, that in the process they were being unkind to poor Aimoni whom we ostracised for most of our childhood years and, by and large, ignored thereafter. The rest of us cousins had each other for company, she only had her swing – fixed for her by her father not long before he was killed and she lost everything but her life and that grotesque toothy smile.

Pehi was grateful for the swing. So long as Aimoni was on it, she did not have to worry about her and could go about doing her own work – cutting thread, weaving clothes on order, pounding rice for other people's homes. And Aimoni had not come in her way for the last eighteen years. Except for the time when she broke her leg and was in bed for three months.

Nobody would have noticed the broken bone as Aimoni anyway walked with a slight limp since that night so many years ago. In any case, she could not say anything to express her pain. But *pehi* noticed the swelling under her *mekhala* one day while giving her a bath. When they took her to the Civil Hospital, the X-ray showed a broken femur. With the plaster cast the doctor made for her, Aimoni was in bed for three months. *Pehi* took to complaining with renewed vigour about how 'this girl' had gone and got her leg broken, and she had to stand guard over her so that she did not try to get out of bed and make things worse. As it is, she had to slave to make ends meet, and now because of 'this girl' again, she was falling behind on her weaving orders.

Aimoni only smiled. The incompetent doctor at the Civil Hospital had joined her bone at a strange angle so that she would never be able to stand straight again. But even when she had to literally drag herself to the swing every morning after the plaster had been removed three months later, she smiled.

The smile was still there on her face the day they had to bring her down by cutting the rope around her neck. She had used the swing as a noose – nobody knew how she had managed to do that.

Now there is no swing in the backyard.

I DO NOT LOVE SAM

It was hard not to love Sam. For twelve years, I thought I was in love with him before I could finally admit to myself that I had always loved the idea of Sam, never Sam himself. He was everything that was beyond reach, everything forbidden. Insisting on loving him was my way of rebelling against the norms of my family, the education system that tried to mould my character and the society that governed my choices. But I was not to know all this until much later. And when I did, my rebellion began to seem quite pointless.

When I first saw Sam, I was twelve. I was the brightest student in class, he was the son of the school gardener. In our residential school run by Catholic nuns, it was drilled into us that even looking at boys was a sinful act. The patron saint of our school was a young girl who had killed herself rather than be 'kissed' forcibly by a boy – or so we were told euphemistically. We could not wear short skirts – they had to cover our legs down to our calves. We could not wear short socks – they had to cover our feet up to our calves. We had to wear pristine white shirts, preferably with full sleeves. Hair tied in red ribbons, nails short and clean, no flashy jewellery. "They might as well make us wear those bulky habits," the girls often complained.

But it wasn't just the dress that they found so constraining. We had very little contact with the outside world, and our everyday lives were governed by a strict routine that was supposed to keep our minds away from sinful thoughts. We were trained to see God and his divine message in everything; even our extra-curricular activities revolved around God Almighty. From our singing classes to dramatics to work experience to physical education, everything was aimed at equipping us to find the morality and divinity within us.

Being at the age that we were, attaining godliness was of course not among the priorities in life for most girls. Besides, most were extremely resentful of all the restraints imposed upon them by the school. But our parents had deemed such discipline necessary for the development of our characters and had thus sent us to this school. Girls, their middle class background dictated, should learn virtuous living and moral values. The Catholic nuns could drill that into us. Being educated in an English medium school would also give us an edge in life and ensure we got good, secure jobs; or at least marry good men with secure, stable jobs.

Our school was among the best in Assam. Its reputation was such that even parents with die-hard rightist leanings conveniently suspended their inherent mistrust of Christian institutions and were willing to make huge donations to get their girls admitted. And it is true that we were given an excellent education: our school alumni consisted of very prominent citizens. It was every parent's dream to see their girls ascend the same heights.

My parents had also sent me there with the same intention. They were happy when I started coming first in class, and also excelling in most extra-curricular activities. I loved singing and dramatics, and no school play was complete without me. I also wrote the occasional poem which I would send home to my father. A writer himself, it would make my father very proud to send his daughter's poetry to the local magazines and newspapers and see it published. Every time one of my poems got published, I would find a special mention in the morning assembly in Mother Superior's address. I was the teachers' pet – never getting into any trouble, always seemingly a stickler for rules. In other words, I always came through as the perfect conformist, unlike most girls my age.

Quite a few of my classmates who regularly broke curfew to read adult magazines under torchlight at night, or earned repeated reprimands for wearing their socks rolled down, did not like me much. They could never believe that even I found the school rules constraining, or that even I wished I could sometimes roll up the sleeves of my shirt, or not have to brush my shoes every morning. I did not always want to sing hymns in singing class, or play the virtuous husband in the school play. I rather enjoyed playing Faustus and selling my soul to the devil, the one time that we performed Marlowe.

But I never rebelled outwardly like the other girls. My rebellions were always silent – like when I wrote about carnal love in some of my poems. If the Sisters had seen some of my poems before they were published, they would have burnt them – or me – at the stake. But once the poems had been published in reputed journals, they could do very little but praise me for the good publicity I gave to the school in the outside world. My biggest rebellion, however, was falling in love with Sam.

I saw Sam for the first time, one day, when I was returning to the dorm after a particularly long practice session for a school play. I rather fancy it was *Doctor Faustus* because it would fit in perfectly with the theme of selling my soul to the devil, but I cannot really be sure now, so many years down the line. He and his father were not allowed out in the school grounds till teaching hours were over, and the girls had returned to the dorm for lunch. They worked in the garden for a few hours thereafter, till it was time for the girls to come out for their evening stroll led by one of the Sisters, forming a straight line, hands behind their backs. They could not talk among themselves or they would find themselves faced with the most ignominious command of all, 'Finger on your lips'!

Sister Theresa, who had always been particularly fond of me, had held me back that day after everybody else had left. She was walking me back to the dorm still discussing some lines, when I nearly stumbled and fell over Sam who was weeding one of the flower beds along the way. After we exchanged apologies, Sister Theresa introduced me to Sam and his father, and as we continued on our way to the dorm, she told me how they had come to live on the school grounds.

During the ethnic riots in Barbari, when the Bodo and

Adivasi villagers had attacked each other, Sam's family had lost everything, including the mother and two sisters. With very little government aid forthcoming to properly rehabilitate the people affected by the riots, a few Catholic organisations had come forward to help them. After the government-run relief camps had closed down, the displaced people had been forced to go out looking for alternative places to stay. The Adivasis were the worst affected; most of them had lost their land and did not possess any other livelihood skills to sustain themselves economically. When the school building, that had housed them immediately after the riots, was once again used for teaching, the Catholic organisations arranged for alternative accommodation for those who approached them. Many opted to convert to Christianity so that they could get employment in Christian organisations and institutions.

Shyamkanu Murmu's father offered his son up for conversion while he himself adamantly retained the faith of his ancestors. And after Shyamkanu became Sam, father and son both came to stay in our school and work as gardeners. When the Sisters saw that Sam was very bright, they began to take a keen interest in his education as well. Now Sister Theresa and a few other nuns gave him regular lessons, and Sam had impressed them all with his sharp mind and quick intellect. They had high hopes of training him for priesthood and sending him back someday among his people to preach the word of Christ.

As Sister Theresa narrated all this to me, I do not mind admitting that my first reaction was a feeling of being privileged. Nobody in school ever treated any of the girls as adult enough to tell them about the harsher realities of life. And here was this old nun who did not mind shaking me up a little with tales of such horrors. Did she really think I was mature enough to handle the truth?

At the same time, I was also seized by a sense of self-pity at how little I knew about the outside world. There was so much going on out there, so many people were suffering, so many upheavals were taking place every day, but I was ensconced in a protective cocoon and had no access to any of it. None of it affected me, whereas people like Sam had seen so much and been through so much, their life experiences must have enriched them in a way that I could never hope for myself.

Immediately as I thought this, however, I remembered the pain that such experiences must have brought with them – the loss of family, of home and hearth, of kith and kin, of everything familiar and things held dear. And I felt ashamed of my own thoughts.

For a long time afterwards, I kept trying to bump into Sam once again, intending to somehow make up for my initial insensitive reaction to his story. After many abortive attempts, I approached Sister Theresa herself with a bold proposal. I went up to her and honestly admitted that I could not help thinking about what she had told me about Sam. I told her I wanted to help him in some way, and perhaps I could assist her during the lessons she gave him?

"Silly child!" Sister Theresa laughed benignly. "Give him lessons? He is two classes ahead of you already, and maybe four or five years elder to you. Why, he could give *you* lessons if you wanted."

"But he looks so small, Sister."

"He does, doesn't he? That's what hunger and deprivation does to you, child. They were never well off to begin with, and then the riots took away whatever little they did have. He is a handsome boy, although so dark like all his people. Let him stay here for another year and he will grow big and strong and then you will not recognise him at all," she laughed again.

Indeed, as Sister Theresa had predicted, Sam's bony structure soon filled up with strong muscles and his dark skin was stretched tight against his frame. I used to watch him sometimes, on the sly, from the dorm window as he worked in the garden, and fancied I could see his sweat gleaming in the sun, his skin shining. At night, I would dream of running my hands over his glistening body, his tongue licking my skin in return, and wake up sweating and shaking from guilty passion.

During the day, whenever I met him, I would fervently hope that his sharp eyes could not penetrate my soul and uncover my secret fantasies. I would meet him quite often now, thanks to Sister Theresa who had, after all, arranged for me to give him Axamiya and Hindi lessons, neither of which the nuns could manage. Our regular Axamiya and Hindi teachers could not spare the extra time required, and these were the two languages Sam had to learn if he was to function in the society outside of the school. After the initial few lessons, it was no longer me teaching Sam, but the two of us learning together, sitting under the big krishnasura tree in the school yard most afternoons. But neither of us complained. We had become fast friends now.

Sam was a great story teller, telling me about his old life in the village, his old school which only had half walls and no benches, where stray cattle walked in and out of the classrooms with no doors during lessons. We would laugh then, and I would wonder how Sam could be so matter-of-fact about it all. I thought I would have felt bitter and deprived if I ever had to study in such a school. Then I would contrast the closed environment of our school with the wall-less, door-less school Sam had gone to and wonder at the disparity.

Sometimes Sam also told me about his mother who was killed in the riots: how she would hum old, nearly forgotten folksongs under her breath, as she went about sweeping the front yard or making frescoes of mud and cowdung on the walls of their tiny hut. She would watch over his father as he got drunk every evening with friends and neighbours, who would have come to taste the best *haria* in the village that she made. They never had plenty, but she always managed to keep her three children well-fed and happy. Then his eyes would burn with hatred towards an unseen enemy when he spoke of his sisters whose dead bodies were recovered in the jungle two days after their village had been burnt down. At those times, I would feel like I was looking into his soul, uncovering the real person he was.

Sam was not the school gardener's son, Sam was not the future priest the nuns were hoping to see him grow into. Sam did not belong to the Church which had taken him in and had such high hopes from him. He was also not the man who came to me now, almost every night, in my dreams and fuelled my latent desires. He did not belong to me either, and although I knew this with a certainty, I vowed to love him forever; like I loved him then, and for the four years he lived in our school. Even when he left to complete his Higher Secondary studies in Guwahati, and I had to stay back in school without him for two years, I continued to love him silently, rebelling silently.

I was rebelling against dear kind Sister Theresa who always said I was the most compassionate girl she had ever seen, and how Christian it was of me to care about the less fortunate. I never thought Sam was less fortunate; for me, he was always richer for his life experiences. I was also rebelling against my parents who would never deem a poor village boy, non-Axamiya at that, deserving of my affections in any way. I always thought I was the poorer person, having nothing to offer but the false middle class values I had grown up with, and a shallow morality that had no place in real life.

No, Sam did not belong there under that krishnasura tree. He belonged back in his village, among his people. One day, I knew, he would go back.

* * *

A thousand different emotions were chasing around inside me as I dialled the mobile number scribbled on my grimy notebook. *Shyamkanu Murmu (Sam) 9864074837.* The look he gave me the last time I saw him, two years back, should have deterred me from making this call. I knew what he thought of me – and it wasn't flattering. Why then was I calling him again now? What did I have to prove to him? Why did I have to prove anything to him at all anyway?

The Sam I knew had turned into somebody else when I met him in Guwahati after I left school to join B Baruah College for my BA. Out of the protective school environment, I learnt some very harsh lessons. One was that I was nobody special; there were hundreds, if not thousands, of other talented and intelligent people everywhere, many of them much more talented and intelligent than I could ever be. Which is why I did not get admission into Cotton College where all the bright students go. Sam, though, had easily got admission there – he was exceptional when I knew him in school and spent so many afternoons in his company; he continued to be exceptional in the intervening years that I barely saw him except for a few brief visits he paid his father and the nuns while school was still in session for us.

During those years, I would write to him regularly, tell him silly little details about my daily life, send him cuttings of my published poems, ask him for his opinion, beg him to tell me about his life in the hostel, the city, the outside world. His replies, whenever they came, were very brief and never warm towards me. They would, however, be full of invective against the 'oppressors' and the 'bourgeoisie', and about the need for the rise of the 'proletariat'. His passion for communist literature fuelled mine, and I would spend hours reading about Marx and Engels in the school library. Very little else was available in the limited collection in our library.

By the time I left school and joined college though, I

learnt that Sam had moved on from the communist ideology and was now talking of self-determination and ethnic identity and nationalism and the need for retribalisation. He spoke passionately about his ancestors, who had been brought to Assam from Chota Nagpur by the British, to work in the tea gardens or to cultivate the wastelands. They had stayed back since they first arrived in the nineteenth century and had embraced the local culture and language. But they were never accepted here, and they would always remain the pariahs unless they stood up for themselves.

So Sam renounced Christianity, much to the disappointment of the nuns who, nonetheless, continued to shelter his father in the school. He also changed back his name to Shyamkanu Murmu through an affidavit in the High Court.

"They cannot make us forget our roots forever. Such conspiracies never work for too long. We have been fools, but now we know that if we are to survive, we have to reclaim our lost identity," he would declare between puffs of post-coital cigarettes, for we had now taken to sleeping together often in his dingy hostel room, away from the watchful eyes of the nuns and my parents' moral injunctions.

"Yes, but what's changing your name got to do with it?" I would ask.

"The personal is political, Jonali. The personal is political," he would announce gravely, expelling more smoke through the lips that had tugged at my breasts not long ago.

And once again, I found myself trying to keep up with him. I would never miss a single Political Science class and looked forward to taking up Sociology for my MA:

our college did not offer Sociology at the BA level. What I could not look forward to, however, was to ever belong to Sam or for him to ever belong to me.

Once when I started talking about a future together with him, his whole body had stiffened. I could feel his muscles bunch up under my cheek as I lay with my head on his shoulder. He never held me after sex, I never wanted to let go. He withdrew into another world, I into his.

"We do not have a future together, Jonali. I thought I had made that clear from the very beginning." He never had, but I could not open my mouth to correct him just then. "We both enjoy each other's company, and that's all we can share. I have never made any false promises to you, so you cannot hold anything against me."

True, he had never promised anything. But didn't having sex mean anything? Didn't holding another person, sleeping together, talking together, being together amount to anything? Didn't so many years of friendship and closeness mean anything, lead anywhere? Apparently not for Sam, and as I valiantly swallowed my pride and my hurt, I remembered the resolve I had made so many years ago in school to love him no matter what. I had accepted then that I could not have him to myself, I reconciled myself again now to the fact that there were certain things that were greater than the individual – like one's ethnicity, one's own people and one's ideology. I wanted desperately to reason with Sam that our being together should make no difference to his identity and his ideology; that I could be his partner in his fight to get his people their due because I empathised; and that if we ever got married, it would be the perfect politics born out of the union of two individuals from the two communities at the extreme ends of the ethnic hierarchy.

"It would set a precedent," I had said desperately on the eve of my departure for Delhi, where my parents were sending me to study Sociology as I had wished, and to keep me away from Sam as they thought fit, after they discovered I was still seeing him.

That was when he had given me a look of utter contempt. "You and your people are all the enemy," he had said and walked away.

And now I was back, after nursing a deep wound for nearly two years, and a void inside me that nothing had been able to fill – not a new place, not new friends, not new ideas, not new preoccupations. I had tried everything, but I could not let go of Sam, despite the hurt he had given me. I ran into an old college mate of Sam's a few days after returning from Delhi, and he told me that Sam had joined politics soon after college. That came as no surprise to me. He said that, for a while, he had been the rising star in the Adivasi community and it had been predicted that he would go far in state politics. Once again, that was something I had always expected. The college mate had followed Sam's career through the newspapers where he would be mentioned quite often.

"I ran into Sam about a year ago and saved his number on my mobile. You can have it, although I am not sure if it is still functional. I have never tried to contact him on it. For you, that's the least I can do," he said meaningfully, because he had known how much in love I had been with Sam.

When I first tried the number he gave me, and nobody picked up the phone at the other end, I was almost relived. But instinctively, I redialed, and the voice that answered was unmistakably Sam's. He sounded drunk, and it was 11 o' clock in the morning. Or maybe he had been sleeping, I thought as I said, "Sam?"

"Jonali?!" He sounded surprised and bemused.

"Yes, it's me. I am back. Where are you?"

"You know, I really don't know."

"What do you mean you don't know, Sam?" I realised I had come out more strongly than I intended.

"I was at a party last night... Our local MLA, you know... Great man... He personally invited me. I am his right hand man. He cannot win elections without me. He has promised me a ticket next time round. Then I will also be a minister. Then everybody will know what this Shyamkanu Murmu is all about! You, your nuns and your people, and everybody else who always looked down upon me, pitied me, took me in so that you could feel great about yourselves. You will know..."

He was still blubbering on when I hung up. For the first time in all the twelve years that I had known Sam, I did not feel any pain at what I heard him say. I only felt regret for a boy who had had everything despite losing so much, and pity for a man who had everything by the sound of it, but had lost himself, perhaps forever. I, on the other hand, suddenly found myself healed and whole. And I could finally say to myself, and to anyone who cared to know, that I did not love Sam anymore.

MELKI *BURI*

It was perhaps the greatest irony I have ever seen in life: that Melki *buri* should die dumb. While alive, she was all about *mel mara* – talk, talk, talk, gossip, gossip, gossip. But for days before she died, she lay on her deathbed without speaking a word. And just as silently, she passed away. To all those who knew her, and were used to her – nobody loved her – Melki *buri* effectively died the day she stopped talking. While alive, she would talk incessantly about everybody she ever knew or wanted others to think she knew. Whether anyone wanted to hear her stories or not, she would also talk non-stop about everything she ever did or thought about doing or, at least, thought she could do. Nobody ever wanted to cross her path because that would mean having to listen her for at least a half hour. If you were smart, you would not listen to her at all but nod at intervals while conjuring, with half a mind, schemes to escape her; the other half of your mind might very well be dreading how you would appear in her tale about you to the next person.

Thankfully, however, we did not have to tolerate *buri* throughout the year. For months on end, she would lock up her tiny thatched hut and go away from the village, wandering around god knows where, doing god knows what, but always bringing back stories of people and places we might just have heard of, but never thought to see. Her hut, and the small patch of land it was built on, was all she had; she had no agricultural land, no known source of livelihood. Strangely, it seems, Melki *buri* never needed any money to travel but whenever she returned, she would have enough to sustain her till her next wandering. She would stay in the village for only as long as this mysteriously acquired money lasted.

Xarbbe and his gang of idlers were the only people in the village who ever willingly stopped to talk to Melki *buri*. And then too, it was to laugh at her; not because they had any regard or concern for her. But *buri* was always too self-involved to notice them sniggering behind her back, and would regale them with her tales every time they stopped her in the village square outside Naren's store, which was their regular *adda*. Sometimes, however, if they were too engrossed in their carom game or cards, and *buri* wanted to talk to them, they would throw stones at her and chase her away. She would scream abuses at them at the top of her voice and curse them all the way to her house, but would return again the next day if they wanted to listen to her then.

It was Xarbbe who told everyone in the village the story of Melki *buri's* visit to Jagannath Dham a couple of years back. She had left the village and gone to Guwahati by bus. When the conductor demanded that she pay her fare, she ticked him off saying,

"One does not ask for fares from a *tirtha-jatri*. I am

going to Puri Jagannath and when I am there, I shall pray for you. Let that be your payment."

In Guwahati, she boarded a second class compartment in the train to Puri, and settled down on the floor near the toilet with the small bundle of clothes that she always carried on her travels. If anybody tried to chase her away, she would show them the fear of God and they would end up giving her money instead, to help her on her "last journey of life" to the sacred place. In this way, she had amassed enough to not only sustain herself in Puri but to return in style after visiting all the temples there, on a paid second class train berth.

We were all amazed at her resourcefulness but nobody said anything to her face for fear of having to listen to other such tales. Second hand accounts from Xarbbe and his gang were good enough for us. We knew she must be extremely inventive in order to be able to travel around on no money at all. And then, it was some feat to come to no harm while traversing the entire length and breadth of the state – as she claimed, and Xarbbe attested it was true – when militants were roaming around everywhere and the police-military were hunting them down and killing civilians. Every time she was gone for a long stretch, there were many in the village who would start speculating that maybe she was dead.

"Nothing can silence her but a machine gun," they would say, almost hopefully.

"She could herself kill a few military men with her machine-gun mouth," others would add and then, they would all laugh.

Melki *buri* always came back though. Nothing seemed to faze Melki *buri*.

Once Xarbbe had asked her what she lived on during her travels, where she slept, what she ate. She had replied that she had friends almost everywhere she went. Where she had none, she made new ones. She regaled them with her stories and, in return, they gave her food and shelter.

"This old Melki is a regular travelling saleswoman of stories," she would say, and laugh through the remnants of her *tamul*-stained teeth.

"Who would buy your stories, *buri*? Nobody likes them," the loafers would taunt.

"How would you know? Didn't you just pay for my tea and give me *tamul* while I was narrating my travel stories to you? There are many like you – you may think you don't want to hear my stories, you may make fun of me behind my back. But the things I have seen and the places I have gone to, you babies know nothing about. If I squeeze your lips now, your mothers' breast milk will come pouring out – but this Melki has seen life. Yes, I have seen everything. What have you seen? What do you know?"

"*Hobo ja, buri*. Go get lost! You've got your tea and your *tamul*, now leave. *Sei*!"

And Melki *buri* would laugh, throw a few more abuses their way, and walk away happily.

Despite her claims of having friends all over the place, though, nobody in the village had seen anybody ever come to visit Melki *buri*. All her family members had died one by one during a cholera epidemic that had struck our village many years ago, leaving her all alone. She had not turned to anyone for help then, and she did not ask anybody for anything now. She owed nothing, gave nothing. Nobody loved her, and she had no kind words to say about anybody either. Once she had taken to travelling, she had continued doing so, and there was nobody in the village to ask her not to, or to caution her about the dangers of a woman travelling alone. Nobody cared, but she always seemed to manage quite well on her own. Until, of course, one day, when she collapsed.

The line bus had just dropped her off in front of Naren's store, and before she could take a few steps from under the *ahat* tree at the bus stop, Melki *buri* fell down in a heap. Naren saw her from inside his store and shouted out to the idlers, "*Oi* Xarbbe! Xarbbessar *oi*! *Buri's* dead! Run, run, go to her. See what happened."

He also made his way with a mug of water to the motionless old woman as quickly as he could, and helped Xarbbe and his gang lay her down on the wooden bench at the bus stop. *Buri* came to when they sprinkled some water from the mug on her face. But when she opened her mouth to say something, no words came out, not even a sound. Melki *buri*, the terror of our village, whose talkative nature had given her the name three generations of our village knew her by, had lost her voice. Nobody knew how, nobody knew why. If the old woman could talk, she would have had a ready tale, but she had been silenced, for all we knew then, forever.

The young men carried her to her hut and placed her on her bed where she lay, till she died. She could not move any part of her body except her eyes, and they were filled with terror. Was it the terror of the thing that had caused her illness? Or was it the terror of finally not being able to fend for herself?

The women of the village took turns cooking for her and feeding her and everybody forgot their fear of her and came to look in on her every now and then. So long as Melki *buri* was independent, she had nobody. Nobody could tolerate her, they laughed at her and avoided her. But now that she was voiceless and helpless, the entire village united to take care of her. True some of them did still laugh about her plight, threading wild stories about what had caused Melki to be deprived of her power for *mel mara*, but nobody was malicious towards her anymore. Even Xarbbe and his gang moved their *adda* from outside Naren's store to Melki *buri's* house to keep her company.

"*Oi buri!* After you are dead we will occupy your house, do you know that? We will make this our youth club. We also need someplace to get together, no? You can come back and haunt us all you want and tell us your stories again," they would joke with her. Melki would just lie there, but the look in her eyes would soften a little.

One morning, Naren had come to see her with a cup of tea. When he tried to lift her head to pour the tea into her mouth, he found her body cold. Immediately, he alerted everybody in the village. The whole village gathered around Melki *buri's* bed. A council was held to decide how to perform her last rites since she had no known family. In the end, Xarbbe came forward to light her pyre. They cut down some bamboo from *buri's* backyard to build a *sangi* to carry her to the river bank for cremation. The old woman, who had been shunned by everybody in life, was now joined by almost the entire village in her last journey.

Naren was the last one to turn his back on the old woman's body after she had been placed on the pyre prepared by the idlers' gang. He would forever afterwards tell the story of the terror he felt when he heard a faint humming sound behind him, as if the dead woman had found her voice again. He had slowly turned around to make sure he was not hallucinating. All he saw, however, was a bee hovering over Melki *buri's* lips.

ANDOLAN*

Our Barbari is a small town with a big population. Over the years, it has grown into a sufficiently important commercial hub of the kind that dots most of mofussil Assam. Like most of these mofussil towns, Barbari is also not particularly well known outside its own district, but it does constitute an indispensable part of the intricate local commercial network. The reasons Barbari developed its commercial nature are many – for one, we have a small sized tea garden right outside town. Or to put it more correctly, our town grew up around this small sized tea garden, Kalguri, which had retained the original name of the area it was built on. My father was among the few educated middle class Axamiya people employed by the British owners of the garden to work as babus in the garden office. Most of the rest of the middle and lower rung white collar employees were East Bengalis, who were content to live in the quarters provided for them by the tea garden owners and the not-so-meagre salaries paid to them. Each garden was like a fortress in itself, where tight security

* Agitation

and adequate isolation from the outside world ensured the safety, not just of the white masters, but also of the expensive factory equipment and priceless tea plantation during a period of political turmoil and growing anti-colonial sentiments. Such isolation suited the Bengali *babus* well as they were also considered outsiders, in a land where middle class and grassroots level passions were building up against immigrants like them who had been imported by the white masters and given preference in matters of employment over the local people.

It was constricting, however, for the Axamiya employees like my father. They soon ventured out of the confines of the garden and started reclaiming the plentiful forest and waste lands surrounding the plantation. Eventually, they became masters of vast tracts of land, virtual zamindars. When they had had their fill, they brought people from their native villages in other parts of Assam and gave them land and settled them in the area which then came to be known as Barbari. To work on their immense land holdings, these newcomers employed the local tribal population who had been living in the area even before the tea garden had been set up. These were mostly Bodo people who had been employed by the tea garden owners before it was decided that it would be cheaper to get indentured labourers from other tribal areas in mainland India. The Bodo labourers were hard working, but, according to their employers, often intractable. Besides, since they had their own agricultural land to fall back upon, they could not be coerced to stay against their will if they wanted to leave.

The new labour force subsequently imported comprised

of poverty-stricken tribals from Central and Eastern India who were bought and sold like cattle by and for the British plantation owners. They were made to live virtually like slaves within the tea garden complex under inhuman conditions, and it continued this way for generations. A few very lucky ones among them had been relieved from, or allowed to leave, their garden jobs for various reasons. But they had nowhere to go – their original homeland was a forgotten dream for most of them – and they opted to settle down in the areas surrounding Barbari. Eventually, these *baganiya* or ex-tea tribals, as they came to be called, set up their own villages in the area. Some of them managed to reclaim some land while others were employed by the people of Barbari in various capacities as household or agricultural help.

This small *baganiya* population could not, however, meet the huge demand for agriculturists in the vast amounts of land reclaimed by my father and his peers. And although a few Bihari and Nepali people had also heard of the new opportunities cropping up in the area, and had come to Barbari looking for employment, the work force was still not enough. So, they decided to allow migrant peasants from East Bengal to come and settle in the region. Most of these peasants were poor and landless, and eager to move to any place that offered them an opportunity to till the soil. Equally unwelcome as their white collar compatriots, they were nonetheless tolerated by the upper and middle classes because of their potential as agricultural labour. Besides unlike those in the white collar jobs, these peasants were also open to subsuming their native language and culture in the local, and to adopt the way of life of the local population. Their aim was economic survival – they had left behind their original homes in search of land and livelihood, both of which had been in short supply. There was no going back, and if that meant that they would have to accept the lowest rung in the social hierarchy of their adopted homes, they were willing to do so. There was still, however, the problem of their religion.

"Deka, these peasants are Muslims. How can we allow them to settle here? We will be accused of harbouring enemies of our faith," many of the people of Barbari had said when my father had first mooted the possibility of bringing in Muslim peasants.

"Don't worry," my shrewd father had replied. "There are ways of dealing with these *miyas.* They are not like the Hindu Bengalis; they will not try to prove they are superior to us. They will be subservient, and if we are tactful, we can control them. Besides, they will live in their own clusters and villages. We need not worry about their religious customs vitiating our environment."

My father had thus convinced them, and they had allowed him to approach Aminul *mama* to bring some of his people to settle near Barbari. He brought them in hordes. Soon we had quite a few *miya* villages in the area. They began working in our fields, and Aminul *mama* also employed quite a few of them himself. Aminul *mama* was an East Bengali *matabbar* – a community leader of sorts – who had settled down in Kalguri, a few kilometers from Barbari, when the first wave of peasant migration from East Bengal had started under the active encouragement of the British. Some said he had been in the area even before the tea garden had been set up. Others like the Marwari *mahajan*, Moti, claimed he had grabbed his immense tracts of land around the same time that the tea garden was set up.

That was also when the three Marwari merchants of the Barbari-Kalguri area, including Moti himself, had set up shop, selling daily essentials to the tea garden labourers, factory workers and officers. Gradually their businesses had grown so that now they operate not only the rice and sugar mills in the area – the raw materials for which came from Aminul *mama*'s fields and the fields owned by my father and the other Axamiya people of Barbari – but also a garment shop, a small hotel and a tiny cinema hall with an ancient projector. Not long after, a couple of *mitha paan* shops were set up by a few adventurous Bengali Hindus who turned up after hearing about the economic niches being created as the new township began to develop. They continued venturing into Barbari looking for newer avenues, and soon we had a Bengali homeopath, our only doctor in town; a Bengali jewellery maker who soon became the craze of all the women; and a Bengali cycle mechanic.

All these people made up the total population of Barbari and its surrounding areas. As a result, our town took on quite a cosmopolitan character by the time we were born. People from all the communities lived in the same town and sometimes, people from the nearby villages also began to move in as and when their economic conditions improved. As the population grew, so did the need for infrastructure.

A cooperative market and, after that, a cooperative bank were also built up. Not long after independence, a panchayat office was also set up and my father was panchayat president for many years running. He was the undisputed leader of the community, although he was always mindful about including Talukdar *khura*, Aminul *mama*, Rajani *bardeuta*, Shishir *kaku* and all the other prominent people of Barbari in every decision he took.

All these people together took the initiative to approach the district administration first for a primary school, which was later upgraded to an MV school while we were students. Subsequently, it became a High School and today I hear it is a Higher Secondary school. It is to this school that all of us went, whether we were Axamiya or *miya* or Bihari or Bengali or *baganiya* or Nepali. I had friends from all the communities. But none of us had any idea then that we were all studying together there only because we did not have any option. If there had been more than one school in our small town, perhaps the affluent middle class people like my parents would have sent us to one school, and the poorer parents of the tribal and immigrant children would have sent them to another. We would have remained separated then as we were to be separated soon, once we left school, and were slotted into different ranks and files as dictated by prevalent societal norms. Since we were forced together, however, everybody celebrated Bihu and everybody danced to the *dhak* during Durga Puja. When the *baganiyas* had their Kali Puja in December, everybody went to the all night open-air cinema shows held in their *basti.* One year, our school Saraswati Puja president was a *miya*, Aminul *mama's* son, Khairul. We had great fun together, and did not know then that we were any different from each other.

This was the way things were among us children. Among the grown-ups, of course, it was a different story. When Aminul *mama* came home, he knew that he could not come inside and sit in our drawing room. He and my father would discuss their business affairs sitting on the verandah. There was a different cup and saucer kept for him, but at least he did not have to wash them himself before leaving. Others like Abdul *chacha*, who was the president of the cooperative market, but much less powerful than Aminul *mama*, would have to. As would all the Bodo, Nepali, Bihari and *baganiya* visitors to our house – my mother would insist on it.

"Or else," she told my father, "They cannot set foot in my house at all."

Only the Bengali Hindus were considered clean enough to eat from the same plates as us. My mother would often send across food that she had cooked to *kakima* next door. Similarly, whenever *kakima* cooked something she knew we liked, she would call one of us and pass us the food through a gap in the fence. When we visited any of our friends' houses, however, we were never expected to wash our own cups and plates. My mother would never eat in anybody else's house, of course, but we would gladly eat the duck eggs and buffalo milk offered at Khairul's house, or the pigeon meat at Sabita's house – she was a Bodo and the daughter of our school teacher, Ramendra Musahary. Of course, we could not eat the pork they made because that would be against our religion, nor could we eat any kind of meat at our Muslim friends' houses for fear it might be contaminated – they cooked beef in the same utensils, after all. But I came to know later that Akhyay *da* would not only eat pork and beef with his *baganiya* and *miya* friends but also drink the *jou* with his Bodo friends and *haria* with the *baganiyas.* Alcohol was another taboo at home, but it seems all my elder brothers had developed a taste for it early in life. Only so long as my mother did not know, they were safe.

* * *

Once MV school was over, Barbari had nothing left to offer by way of education. My father, however, insisted that all his children should get a proper education and go to university. All my brothers had left home for Guwahati once they had completed MV school in Barbari. Only Akhyay *da* had resisted. He wanted to stay close to home, and so he enrolled in the Kalguri Higher Secondary School and cycled to and from school every day. After scraping through High School, he struggled with his Higher Secondary studies and managed to pass after two attempts. Thereafter, he decided to give up studies altogether, much to our parents' dismay. Eventually he joined the tea estate office once father retired.

I followed my family tradition and left home to join High School in Guwahati. But where none of my older brothers could manage to continue studying beyond college, I even did my MA from Gauhati University. Thereafter, I joined as a lecturer in B Baruah College before getting married. My father insisted that his only daughter, the brightest of his children, should get the best education and then marry somebody intellectually her equal. He found me a professor at the Gauhati University to marry, and with implicit faith in his judgment, I married a man I had barely met twice before I pledged before the sacred fire to be his wife not just in this life, but for quite a few more to come.

My husband was a kind man who did not make me feel the lack of anything. Anything, that is, except his company. After our marriage, he became one of the most well known and widely read folklorists of Assam, and people everywhere sought him out and invited him to meetings and functions and seminars. When he was not attending these meetings and functions and seminars, he was conducting field work in some interior village and writing his research papers. While I was proud of his achievements, I often found myself wishing he would spare some more time for me and the children – we had two and they also missed their father sorely.

"Why don't you take them with you on one of your field visits?" I would often ask. "They will have your company and also learn from seeing the outside world."

"Do you know what these places I go to are like?" He would question me in return. "It is best they do not know this 'outside world' of yours. Do you want them to see how man behaves towards his fellow men in the name of religion and ethnicity? Yes, I study the customs and cultures of these societies, and they are all very beautiful. People appreciate what I write because I write about the richness of each. But

I also see the fear, the paranoia and the hatred they each carry for the other at their core. Why else do you think we had communal riots every decade since independence, Jeuti? No, it is best for them to remain in this sanitised urban environment, where they do not have to get to see or feel any sense of difference from their classmates and friends. Let them continue living in this bubble for as long as they can, for before long, this bubble is going to burst anyway. Mark my words, I have seen it coming, there will be riots everywhere again soon, and violence and genocide. The hatred we have been nursing against each other in our breasts will engulf us soon."

I was too shocked at his outburst to respond immediately, and by the time I recovered he had walked away. There were so many things I wanted to tell him, and so many ways I could set the record straight for him. After all, did I not grow up in Barbari? Did we not all live in harmony there? True, communal and ethnic riots had taken place everywhere else in Assam, but never in Barbari. Though very old now, people like Aminul *mama* and Shishir *kaku* – my father had died a few years back – still led their respective communities. They had always maintained peace in the area even when the neighbouring regions had been in ferment. Barbari would never be like any of the other places of Assam, I strongly believed, and I told him as much that night as I picked up the threads of our unfinished conversation again.

"How long has it been since you were back there, Jeuti?" he asked me calmly.

"Why, we went there just last summer!"

"No, I mean how long has it been since you were really there? As a part of the place and the community? You go there with the children once or twice every year and stay for a few days and visit your relatives and old friends. But do you still belong there? Do you care to find out what lies beneath the surface? And among the friends that you visit, do you still go to Bhikhu's house in the *baganiya basti*? Or to Abdul's house in the *miya* village? Would you even recognise Abdul now if he stood before you with his long beard and chequered *lungi* and three wives? Would you allow Bhikhu into your house here, today, if he were to decide to come and see his old school friend?"

"Maybe, maybe not. But that's not the point. I am not talking about myself. I left that place a long time ago. What I am saying is that you should not think that disparities will always lead to violence. I think I am a better person for knowing and growing up among so many different kinds of people. I just wanted you to take our children with you so that they could also see all the diversity in the world outside. And feel its richness."

"You could have done that all those times we were in Barbari, couldn't you? Learning about the outside world does not always have to be a clinical experience. It should be lived. It should be felt. This morning, I told you what I felt, and I am telling you now, again, that I have also felt the same foreboding of doom in Barbari."

It is true that he knew more about Barbari now than I ever did. Every time we went there, he would only wait for a cup of tea before mounting my father's old bicycle and peddling away into the nearby villages or to the *baganiya basti* with his cloth bag hanging from one shoulder. His constant companions – a notebook and an assortment of pens – were always in the bag. He would only come back home for meals, for he knew my mother would be extremely hurt if he didn't. Sometimes, Akhyay *da* would give him a ride if he was free, and take him to meet newer people. At those times, they would not return till late night, and when they did, they would both be drunk and singing happily. My mother had long reconciled herself to Akhyay *da's* ways. As for my husband, she was too much in awe of his reputation and too smug in the social status that came with having a famous son-in-law, to complain against his drinking alcohol. If anything, she had taken to defending him now whenever I complained.

"He has to work among these people and gather information. How will he do that if he does not sit down with them and take what is offered? As it is these tribals are so hot-headed, they will take offence at the slightest thing. If he said no, and they took it as an insult, how will he write his books?"

"And if he eats beef with the *miyas?* Would you be ok with that too?" I would throw back at her.

"I know my son-in-law. He will never do anything of that sort," she would maintain obstinately.

I was not so sure myself, but there was very little I could do. He was forever away among these people, and even if he did eat the meat they offered or drank alcohol with them, so long as he did not bring those things home, I preferred not to comment. And he never did; so I let it be.

I was not fine, however, with what he was saying now: that Barbari might be heading towards trouble. The children's summer vacations were approaching and although we had skipped Barbari last year to take them to Darjeeling, this year, I determined to go there. My husband was never unenthusiastic about going to Barbari, and so we drove down two days after the vacations started. We had intended the trip to be a surprise for my mother and had not called ahead to inform her. We should have, for we were just a few kilometers from Kalguri when we sensed something was wrong. The roads were lined with armed paramilitary policemen standing guard every few feet, and armoured trucks could be seen here and there. We stopped in front of one of the policemen and asked him what had happened. He said a young *baganiya* boy had been found murdered last night in Kalguri and any day now, ethnic riots were likely to break out.

My husband did not say "I told you so"; he was not that kind of a person. But I suddenly felt my head reeling. Who was this young man, did I know him? Who had killed him? When we reached Barbari, Akhyay *da* was livid.

"Why didn't you call before leaving Guwahati? This whole place has been tense for a while now – we did not want to alarm you, so we said nothing. But we would never have allowed you to come if we had known. As it is, I was thinking of sending Ma, Matu and the kids to Guwahati. But now, with this boy killed, there is no guarantee that violence will not spill on to the highway. How will you go back now? It is bad enough that we are trapped here, and now you have come too!"

That night, as we sat in the courtyard fanning ourselves and talking of the good old days, we found ourselves whispering, although there was nobody to overhear our conversation. Akhyay *da* and my husband had gone to a peace meeting that had been hastily called to bring the warring communities to a dialogue and subsequently, hopefully, to a mutually acceptable settlement that would defuse the tension and prevent bloodshed. Such meetings had worked in the past when my father and his contemporaries had presided over them, and sometimes through reasoning, and sometimes through coercion, brought the parties in conflict to peace.

"Those were the days when these people knew subservience and accepted the authority of people like your father. Today, everyone has rights, everyone needs power, everyone wants to be the leader. How will society function this way? If everybody were to be king, who would rule over whom?"

My mother's tirade suddenly reminded me of a particular incident in school one day. The first class that day was Sanskrit. Shashtri *saar* was our Sanskrit teacher, and everybody was afraid of him. I was late for some reason and was trembling from head to toe as I stood at the door, not daring to open my mouth and ask for permission to enter. But Shashtri *saar* saw me standing there and stopped the lesson.

"*Ah, maharani*, come in, come in! So you decided to grace us with your presence after all!"

I felt like dying but walked in anyway, only to find that there were no empty seats. When he saw me hovering near the wall and realised why, he turned his attention to Bhikhu who was sitting in the front row.

"*Oi lora*, get up. Go stand against the wall and let Jeuti sit."

Bhikhu did not budge. Shashtri *saar* threw his book at Bhikhu and asked him to get up again. He did get up this time and mumbling something under his breath, came towards the wall.

"What did you just say?" Shashtri *saar* asked him.

"Nothing, *saar*."

"How can it be nothing, I heard you say something. Out with it."

"She is late, why punish me?" Bhikhu spoke out tremulously.

When he heard this, Shashtri *saar* flew into a rage and charged at him. He gave him a resounding slap.

"You *coolie* dog! You dare question my authority? Do you know who she is? She is the daughter of the king of this town. If it was not for him, you would not be here studying at all, but picking leaves all your life like your parents and their parents before them. So when I say you need to vacate your seat for her, you need to vacate your seat for her. Do you understand?"

Bhikhu was now quietly standing against the wall, and Shashtri *saar* turned towards me, "You! Why are you still standing there? Come here and sit down. I don't have all day."

As I walked nearer, however, he saw that I was crying. I did not want him to treat Bhikhu like this. After all, he was my friend, and although it hurt to hear him say it, I did realise that he was right in saying that since I was late, I should be the one standing against the wall, not him.

"What's happened to you now? Why are *you* crying? He got the beating, he has to stand against the wall, and you are crying?"

I could not say anything but started bawling now. Finally Shashtri *saar* gave up, and walked out of the classroom. Later, I went up to Bhikhu and apologised, but he turned his back on me.

The other day, my husband had asked me if I would allow Bhikhu to enter my house in Guwahati now if he suddenly showed up. I had to admit I wouldn't. But it was the same Bhikhu for whom I had shed those tears so many years back. What had changed? Nothing, I realised. I could not speak out in protest then and put my foot down in front of Shashtri *saar.* I would not speak out now and admit to my husband that he had been right. That we had sown the seeds of discontent since the very beginning, but wanted to believe we were not to blame. That we had provided the fuel for the fire, they were only lighting the matches everywhere. Even in Barbari.

Akhyay *da* and my husband returned in the wee hours of the morning after they saw that it was futile to try and broker peace. The riots were inevitable. However, the commanding officer of the paramilitary police force had assured them that if we could drive out before sunrise, we should be safely out of the conflict zone by daybreak. Matu *bou,* my sister-in-law, quickly bundled the children together while I helped my mother collect her valuables. Akhyay *da* stayed behind, and the rest of us drove away. As we crossed Kalguri on our way out, I saw smoke coming out from behind a clump of trees a little way off the highway. It might be houses burning – maybe the riots had started already. Or it could be the young man's cremation. I could not shake off the feeling that it was Bhikhu – my old classmate Bhikhu, some other *baganiya* boy named Bhikhu, didn't matter which Bhikhu. Whoever it was, I was responsible for his death, and the many deaths that would follow once we were safely on our way to Guwahati and the riots had started in earnest.

THE HILLS OF HALFONG

I often feel like jumping off the side of the hills into the steep deep green gorge below. I am not suicidal. Indeed, it is precisely at those times when life seems the most worth living, that I feel like jumping off. I do not want to do it just so I can die, or punish somebody, or register my protest against something. I just wish to jump off and feel alive.

Not that I feel dead now. Far from it. I have a healthy normal life by all standards, a good job in the government college here in Haflong, a comfortable salary, moderate lodgings, a family that is far away enough to be missed and not near enough to be a nuisance, and above all, a steady boyfriend who is willing to wait as long as it takes for me to get ready for marriage.

I love it here. The hills of Haflong have adapted quite well to my moods. The day I first arrived, they were blue in keeping with the pain I imagined I felt at leaving Jitudhon, my boyfriend, behind. But by the time I realised that I was actually feeling a kind of freedom and elation in my soul that I had not felt for a long long time, they turned red with the setting sun.

I fell in love with Haflong the moment we entered the gates of the colonial-style Old Circuit House where the college authorities had decided to put me up for a few days, till they could find me proper accommodation in town closer to the college: the Circuit House was a little distance away from the main town. I was treated like a VIP because I had agreed to join the college, and come to teach at a place that most people considered a punishment posting. A number of my male colleagues who were teaching at the private college in Guwahati where I had worked earlier, had turned down the offer, although a government job was not something people said no to that easily. Haflong was, after all, at the center of the Dimaraji Movement, where violent armed insurgent groups were waging a war against the state and against each other. People got killed here every day and so, I had had a tough time convincing my parents to let me come here. My stubbornness had also hurt Jitu, I know, but I was determined to get away. And I did. And oh, what a place to get away to!

After dumping my luggage in the room allotted to me, I walked across the garden and looked down into the deep gorge below. I was captivated – hills had always fascinated me, but the hills of Haflong affected me like none other. The vast tracts of green forests and red earth below seemed to be calling me towards them, telling me to jump into their bosom, feel the beauty, live, live, live, ecstatically! I might even have given in to the impulse if I had not, suddenly, been distracted by the sight of a tiny train belching smoke, chugging up the terrain below. It curved in and out of the greenery, went into tunnels, climbed higher and higher, got lost in smoke, and found its way again as I stood there mesmerised.

After that first day, I would watch the same scenery every day and relive the same emotions and wonder what I had been doing with my life for so long, living away from Haflong. I refused to move to a rented house in Haflong town when the college found me one, and politely requested them to allow me to stay on in the Circuit House. I told them my parents would be more comfortable knowing that their daughter had government accommodation with proper security, in case of any violence. As it is, they were uneasy about my being here and grumbled constantly: couldn't the college have found another Anthropology teacher for their new department? I knew the Government Tourist Lodge in the town had been occupied by the Indian Army, which was not known for its respect for civilian life and women's dignity. So I told them that they would have to put me up there if they insisted on my staying in town and near the college, but a private residence was not an option. They naturally said no to the Tourist Lodge and agreed reluctantly to let me stay on at the Circuit House.

Here, I could be in the midst of all the political turmoil and yet, find detachment. I could be looking desperately for somebody to drop me to the Circuit House in the middle of a working day, when news spread that a sudden *bandh* had been called by one of the insurgent factions and it was no longer safe to be out of doors. But such desperation would only last so long. The hills around me would be so calm and contented that I would already be feeling a kind of peace inside me as I made my way in somebody's car or motorbike through the streets full of people scrambling to get indoors and out of harm's way.

Maybe the hills taught everybody such detachment, because every time the news of something alarming spread, people would scurry all right, but not long thereafter it would be back to business as usual. Sometimes I wondered how people could take living under the shadow of constant violence so casually. Like, for instance, one day, when a bomb went off at the agricultural department's office, and I asked our peon what the commotion was all about.

"It was a small bomb, madam. Not a big one. A personal matter, not political," he shrugged and walked off.

Was it that the shadow of the hills was more overpowering than the shadow of violence? Did they cast their calm on the people they cradled in their breasts, and no matter how much laceration these people could or would inflict upon the hills, the hills would always protect them?

Jitudhon tried his best for a long time to convince me to go back to Guwahati, and when he realised he could not, he got married to somebody else. My parents pleaded with me constantly but they could not convince me either. The hills had cast their spell. I could not leave.

The sound of gunshots echoing on a silent night could not keep me awake, for the sound of the wind embracing the trees outside my window with a sensual caress would lull me to sleep. The memory of blood on the streets of the town would be wiped clean by the white smoke of the train chugging its way up from Lower Haflong. My soul would lift above and beyond all other thoughts as the smoke spiralled higher and higher up to meet the clouds and I would stand there on the edge, watching, waiting, wanting to grow roots and become a tree. And I would forget the reality of violence and conflict that the hills so cleverly concealed in their many crevasses.

I do not think they will ever make me feel so dead as to jump off the cliff only to feel the thrill of life. No, not my hills of Haflong.

THE RAINS COME FROM BEHIND THE CURTAIN

A few centuries ago, we first awoke from a deep dreamless sleep. We saw the world as a beautiful place, so giving, so loving.

It was some time before a few of us took a peek behind the curtain where dreams floated. What lay beyond was a nightmare.

Others among us had entered into a pact with the world and created this nightmare.

When the nightmare threatened to engulf us, we also entered into a contract with the world – we agreed not to look at the world, and those in cahoots with it complied to leave us alone.

Thus we had continued for centuries, and thus I thought I would pass by.

But he jolted me out of my complacence – the naked man in the park.

They said he was mad. All he did the whole day was sit on the pavement and draw shapes and figures on the concrete.

And he laughed the whole day, all by himself.

I knew he was laughing at me, and at all those who had signed the contract. He had not.

I looked at him and marvelled; I looked at his drawings and shuddered.

The world was there, naked. And all its people – distorted, disproportionate, unsightly.

I had known it was like this all along, but it had taken a madman to define it for me.

I was sane. So I had always looked the other way to avoid embarrassing the world.

The madman dared to look straight at it and all its naked, ugly people, to point at them and laugh. He did not turn his back.

So they called him mad and connived to isolate him, so others would not be influenced by him.

But the madman did not care. He only sat and drew.

He knew he need not go in search of kindred souls – they have a way of coming together, these souls.

And when they come together? Do they all sit down and draw?

Would you find me tomorrow on the pavement with the madman? I don't think so.

I don't have the courage yet. I am sane yet.

Where then am I different from the rest of the world? Or am I at all? I like to believe I am not in the cabal.

The rains are though. Last night, they came and washed it all away – the madman's etchings on the pavement.

For days now, I had tried to sidestep them as I walked past them on my way to the institute, only to see them being trampled under desperate feet trying to keep up the façade: nobody likes to be caught in the nude.

The madman only sat down to draw again. The world continued to conspire.

And last night, the rains also conspired with the world. The rains joined hands with the people. The rains washed it all away.

The rains came from behind the curtain.

AFTERWORD

There is a lot of darkness in people's souls. I have seen this darkness as a researcher trying to make some sense – any sense – of the violence and protracted conflicts that have plagued the region I call home: the Northeast. I have also felt this darkness enveloping me and my dear ones in my personal life, when confronted by a monster I thought was the man I loved. So everywhere I have been, all that I have seen, has often been engulfed in this darkness.

And yet, I have also seen light, and I have also felt love. And that is how I have also come to the realisation that what makes us human, in the end, is the capacity to overcome this darkness, within us, around us.

My stories are a lot about the darkness, but they are also about the small sparks of light that do occasionally dispel the demons in our souls. The brief luminosities of love, life, relations, remembrances, penitence and possibilities are, after all, the things that make life worth living.

Even as a teenager trying to make sense of the world, I used to write lugubrious lines about 'the Black' vying with the light in a 'sooty universe'. Many times in later life, growing up, looking for myself, I have found myself desperately clinging on to the edge of the cliff of reason, staring into the deep gorge of nothingness below. But every time, without fail, I have pulled myself together and pulled myself out. I could do that because I knew, that staring into that same pit of nothingness along with me, was the vast blue sky. And the sky never gives up, it goes on and on.

I have thus been egged on, always, by my sincere belief (or hope) that even in the morbid, there is the mundane; and that even in the worst of us, the best of humanity may sometimes manifest itself. My stories, in a way, are a slice of my research into this strange conundrum of human nature and existence. If they have been successful in convincing my readers that, at times, Blackness may also come with its own lambency, or at least, its own toned-down grayness, I will know that I have not been simply deluding myself all along.